THE PUZZLES OF
PETER DULUTH

Richard Webb, 1933   Hugh Wheeler, ca. 1947

Webb and Wheeler, ca. 1949

THE PUZZLES OF
PETER DULUTH

PATRICK QUENTIN

Introduction by Curtis Evans
Postscript by Mauro Boncompagni
Afterword by Joanna Gondris

Crippen & Landru Publishers
Norfolk, Virginia
2016

Cover artwork by Gail Cross

Lost Classics series design by Deborah Miller

Lost Classics logo, adapted from a drawing
by Ike Morgan, ca. 1895

ISBN: 978-1-936363-13-1 (cloth edition)
ISBN: 978-1-936363-14-8 (trade softcover edition)

FIRST EDITION
Printed in the United States of America on acid-free, re-
cycled paper

Crippen & Landru Publishers
P.O. Box 9315
Norfolk, VA 23505
USA
e-mail: crippenlandru@earthlink.net
web: www.crippenlandru.com

CONTENTS

Puzzles for Posterity

Until the publication by Crippen & Landru of *The Puzzles of Peter Duluth*, a collection of short crime fiction by Patrick Quentin, the author, in spite of being one of the most accomplished figures in mid-twentieth-century American crime writing, had remained almost entirely out of print in the English-speaking world for nearly almost a quarter-century. Meanwhile, myriad lesser mystery writers currently are being revived on a large scale, non-specialist publishers having belatedly come to the realization that there is a sizeable reading audience for vintage crime fiction composed by individuals other than Agatha Christie and her sister Crime Queens. Happily, the works of Ellery Queen, Mary Roberts Rinehart and John Dickson Carr—probably the brightest stars in Golden Age American mystery (though Rinehart's career in mystery fiction actually was launched before the onset of the Golden Age)—recently have been reissued, as have those by such shining American lights as Elizabeth Daly, Clayton Rawson, Stuart Palmer, Mignon Eberhart, Rufus King, Craig Rice and Todd Downing. Additionally, mid-twentieth-century psychological suspense fiction by such notable American authors as Charlotte Armstrong, Vera Caspary, Margaret Millar and Elisabeth Sanxay Holding has been reprinted as well, including in the prestigious form of a two-volume set of novels issued by the Library of America, publisher and champion of American hardboiled and noir fiction by such landmark names as Dashiell Hammett, Raymond Chandler, David Goodis and Jim Thompson. Let us hope that Patrick Quentin's impressive body of crime fiction, which spanned three decades, from *Puzzle for Fools* (1936) to *Family Skeletons* (1965), will soon be revived on a large scale as well, and that Patrick Quentin will again take his rightful place as an author, high up in the crime fiction firmament.

With his usual keen insight Anthony Boucher, the dean of American crime fiction critics, wrote fifty-five years ago that "[o]ne of the best possible textbooks on *The Art of Plotting the Detective Story* would be *The Collected Works of Patrick Quentin*....Quentin...is particularly noted for the enviable polish and grace which make him one of the leading American fabricants of the murderous comedy of manners; but this surface smoothness conceals intricate and meticulous plot construction as faultless as that of Agatha Christie." Crippen & Landru's *The Puzzles of Peter Duluth*, which collects all the short crime fiction concerning the adventures of Patrick Quentin's leading series character, gives vintage mystery fans a tantalizing taste of the fine fare to be found at Patrick Quentin's bountiful criminal buffet, which encompasses everything from classic puzzles to manners mystery to nerve-wracking psychological suspense.

For a little over half of the three-decade writing career of Patrick Quentin (from 1936 to 1952), the author's cognomen, which in fact was a pseudonym, concealed the names of two English expatriates, Richard Wilson Webb (1901-1966) and Hugh Callingham Wheeler (1912-1987). The elder man in this deadly duo, Richard "Rickie" Webb, was born at Burnham-on-Sea, Somerset, the youngest of six children of Frederick Charles Webb and Grace Elizabeth Lucas, master and mistress of Oakover, a local girls' school. After completing his education at Winchester College, Cambridge and the University of Berlin, Webb taught Greek in South Africa for a time and also briefly served as Paris correspondent for a British news agency. In 1926 he migrated from Paris to Philadelphia, where he became a research manager and director with a pharmaceutical company, Smith, Kline and French Laboratories (SKF). In this capacity Webb in the mid-1930s was instrumental in the manufacturing and marketing of SKF's hugely successful amphetamine-based Benzedrine inhaler.

The protean Rickie Webb additionally turned his hand to yet another addictive popular stimulant at this time: detective fiction. Before commencing in 1936 his successful collaboration with Hugh Wheeler, for which he is best

known, Webb authored — either solo or in collaboration
with, variously, Philadelphians Martha Mott Kelley (1906-
1998) and Mary Louise White Aswell (1902-1984) — a half-
dozen detective novels under the pseudonym Q. Patrick:
Cottage Sinister (1931), *Murder at the Women's City Club*
(1932), *Murder at Cambridge* (1933), *S. S. Murder* (1933), *The
Grindle Nightmare* (1935) and *Death Goes to School* (1936).
Webb and Martha Mott Kelley, a recent Radcliffe graduate descended from the Quaker abolitionist and feminist
Lucretia Mott and a niece of the progressive social re-
former Florence Kelley, together devised the Q. Patrick
pseudonym by combining "Pat" (for Kelley's nickname
Patsy) and "Rick" (for Webb's nickname Rickie) to make
"Patrick" and then adding the letter "Q" because they
deemed it "the most intriguing letter in the alphabet."
Kelley left "Q. Patrick" after the publication of two well-
received detective novels, whereupon Webb, after publishing *Murder at Cambridge*, for which he drew partially
upon his own student days, teamed with Mary Louise
White, a graduate of Bryn Mawr, who later became, as
Mary Louise Aswell, one of the publishing world's most
influential editors, to produce another detective novel,
the shipboard mystery *S. S. Murder*. He next wrote two
more Q. Patrick mysteries, the memorably grim and
gruesome *The Grindle Nightmare* and his final solo effort,
Death Goes to School. By the appearance of these latter
two novels, however, Webb had found the person who
proved his ideal partner: a prodigiously talented young
Englishman named Hugh Callingham Wheeler.[1]

Hugh Wheeler — about whom readers will learn much
more in his grand-niece Joanna Gondris's fascinating afterword to this volume — was born in London, the son of a Board
of Trade Examiner, and attended Clayesmore School and the

---

[1] In an essay in *Mysteries Unlocked: Essays in Honor of Douglas G. Greene* (McFarland,
2014), Mauro Boncompagni has pointed out that *Death Goes to School*, typically credited to both Webb and Wheeler, in fact is copyrighted by Webb alone and was dedicated
by him alone to his parents, indicating that the novel was a solo effort on Webb's part.

University of London, where he was awarded a BA degree in English with honors in 1932. Having met the visiting Rickie Webb in London, the twenty-one year old Wheeler, on August 2, 1933 embarked, with dreams of an American literary career in his head, with the business executive turned mystery writer aboard the *Norddeutscher Lloyd* on his return to Philadelphia. (Webb's ocean liner mystery *S. S. Murder*, written with Mary Louise White, was published that fall.) By October, Hugh Wheeler was writing to a brother that he and Webb were working together on a "quite pretentious novel," though the "best parts all are Rickie's" (see afterword).

Young Hugh evidently made great strides with his writing, for in 1936, thoughts of "pretentious" novels laid aside for now, he entered into an ambitious commercial partnership with Webb. Not only did the pair intermittently continue the Q. Patrick series of detective novels (six more of them, including the classic *Death and the Maiden* and two *Crimefiles* books, which took the form of case dossiers with all the clues included, were published between 1937 and 1952), but they also introduced two additional mystery series, produced under a new pair of pseudonyms, Jonathan Stagge and Patrick Quentin, the latter pen name obviously a variation on Q. Patrick. Concerning the composition of the novels that the two writers published between 1936 and 1952, Webb devised the plots, upon which Wheeler expansively elaborated. Both men then honed the final drafts as Wheeler typed.

Inveterate travelers, the pair frequently roamed the Caribbean and Latin America together, thereby providing settings for several of their crime novels. Absent a period when the two authors did service in the Second World War (Hugh Wheeler, who had become a naturalized U. S. citizen in 1940, served in the U. S. Army Medical Corps), Webb and Wheeler from 1939 to 1952 resided together in the Berkshires

---

The Grindle Nightmare, on the other hand, has traditionally been credited to both Webb and White, though in fact it too was copyrighted by Webb alone. On the other hand, it seems not unlikely to me that Hugh Wheeler may have been involved with the composition of both novels, even though he received no official credit.

in rural western Massachusetts, first at Hickory Farm in Tyringham and then at Twin Hills Farm in Monterey. Here they did all their writing, Wheeler later declaring that although he frequently visited New York City, "Monterey is the only place where I can really write."

Webb and Wheeler's Jonathan Stagge novels, nine of which appeared between 1936 and 1949, concern the often macabre murder investigations of an amateur sleuth, Hugh Westlake, a widowed New England country doctor with an exhaustingly rambunctious young daughter, Dawn, who usually somehow manages, quite inadvertently, to help her father solve his cases. Although a clever series of novels, the Stagges, like the Q. Patrick tales, never attained the fame of the Patrick Quentin Peter Duluth mysteries, which were frequently reprinted in paperback and occasionally adapted, with mixed success, for the silver screen.

Between 1936 and 1952 Rickie Webb and Hugh Wheeler collaborated on nine Patrick Quentin novels, in all but one of which the lead character is theatrical producer Peter Duluth, who also serves as the narrator of events. (One of the Patrick Quentin books published in this period, *The Follower*, is non-series.) In addition to detailing the murder cases in which Duluth invariably becomes ensnared, the novels depict the producer's various complicated emotional entanglements, the most significant of which is the lasting one with Iris Pattison, the beautiful debutante he meets in the first novel of the series, *Puzzle for Fools* (1936), and marries in the second, *Puzzle for Players* (1938). Over the course of the rest of the series Peter and Iris weather not only murder but personal and marital challenges, including Peter's amnesia (*Puzzle for Fiends*, 1946), Iris's attraction to another man (*Puzzle for Pilgrims*, 1947) and Peter's personal implication in a ghastly murder and adultery scandal (*Black Widow*, 1952).

The first two novels in the Peter Duluth series are classic "puzzles" in form as well as in name, exercises in fair play clueing that were much commended by contemporary reviewers. *Puzzle for Fools* has a setting reminiscent of Jonathan Latimer's hard-boiled detective novel *Murder in the Madhouse*, published a year previously. Having taken too much solace with the liquor bottle in his despair over the death of his wife in a theater fire, producer Peter Duluth has committed himself into a high class sanatorium in the hope of recovering his mental equilibrium. Naturally murder soon strikes, yet it is not Peter but the owner of the sanatorium, the brilliant psychiatrist Doctor Lenz, who solves the mystery, in the course of which Peter meets his future wife, Iris Pattison (like Peter a "guest" at the sanatorium, Iris has been afflicted with depression since the suicide of her father, who suffered severe financial reverses in the stock market crash.) The medical setting of *Fools* allowed Webb and Wheeler to take advantage of the elder man's extensive pharmaceutical knowledge, with the malady of narcolepsy—for the amelioration of which Benzedrine was promoted in the Thirties—playing a role in the tale.

Doctor Lenz is again on hand when death struts upon the stage in the next Peter Duluth novel, *Puzzle for Players*. The psychiatrist is the major backer of a promising new play being produced by Peter, now released from Lenz's sanatorium and engaged to Iris, for whom Peter has secured a part in the play. Highly praised in its day, *Players* remains a superb example of the Golden Age "fair play" detective novel, offering readers not only a cleverly clued puzzle but colorful characters, an appealing theatrical setting and a resolution that includes, if not exactly the romantic peal of church bells, at least a quickie chapel wedding at Elkton, Maryland. The husband and wife act as the crime solvers in the later, Lenz-less mysteries, with the dynamic Iris functioning in every way as Peter's equal (and then some). Along with Frances and Richard Lockridge's Pam and Jerry North, Kelly Roos's Jeff and Hilda Troy and Craig Rice's Jake and Helene Justus, Peter and Iris Duluth are one of the more notable American "mystery couples" from the era of classic crime fiction, though they eventually came to explore some darker criminal spaces than those other, breezier couples.

Six years would pass before the publication of another Peter Duluth novel, but in the interim there appeared, in *The American Magazine* in 1941, a pair of Peter Duluth novelettes, "Death Rides the Ski-Tow" and "Murder with Flowers," both of which are collected in this volume. Intriguingly kaleidoscopic affairs reminiscent of Alfred Hitchcock films, the two tales find Peter and Iris tasked with untangling some truly outré murder plots. "Death Rides the Ski-Tow" begins bizarrely with a desperate blonde handing Peter a telltale hotdog, while "Murder with Flowers," which opens with Peter and Iris rumbaing at the Opal Room in celebration of their first wedding anniversary, concerns cryptic messages about red and white roses and an elephant that never forgets.

In 1944 Webb and Wheeler expanded "Murder with Flowers" as *Puzzle for Puppets*, the first in a brilliant flurry of Peter Duluth novels that appeared between 1944 and 1952. Both *Puppets* and a later Duluth novel, *Puzzle for Fiends* (1946), are somewhat reminiscent of the noir fiction of Cornell Woolrich, with Peter and Iris, now a Hollywood film star, desperately scampering around San Francisco trying to prevent a series of murders in *Puppets*, and Peter afflicted with amnesia and unwittingly embroiled in a murder plot in *Fiends*. Also rather noirish is *Puzzle for Pilgrims* (1947), winner of France's *Grand Prix de littérature policière* for best foreign crime novel, in which the murder plot is skillfully intertwined with the painful marital problems of the Duluths; *Run to Death* (1948), a superlative hunter-and-hunted tale, evocatively set, like *Pilgrims*, in Mexico; and *Black Widow* (1952), wherein Peter finds himself suspected of adultery and murder. In contrast, *Puzzle for Wantons* (1945), a tale set in Reno, Nevada, divorce capital of the world, is more of a manners mystery, with one of Patrick Quentin's most intricate plots and some delightfully satirical writing.

"Puzzle for Poppy" (1946), included in this volume, is the lone piece of Peter Duluth short fiction that Webb and

Wheeler produced in this period. First published in *Ellery Queen's Mystery Magazine*, "Poppy" is a classic example of the deductive mystery in miniature at which the master himself, Ellery Queen, so excelled. Detailing Peter and Iris's determined efforts to foil a murder plot against the life of a loveable—and extremely wealthy—St. Bernard named Poppy, "Puzzle for Poppy" was aptly dubbed a "delightfully wacky yarn" by Frederic Dannay, editor of *Ellery Queen's Mystery Magazine* and one half of Ellery Queen.

By the publication of the tension-filled *Black Widow* in 1952, Rickie Webb was fifty-one years old and already in declining health. (Photos of Webb taken around this time show him appearing worn and older than his years, while Wheeler, just on the right side of forty, remained boyishly handsome.) That year Webb retired from the lucrative collaboration he had started sixteen years earlier with Wheeler and moved to France, leaving his protégé the farmhouse in the Berkshires and the Patrick Quentin name. Rickie Webb would pass away fourteen years later, at the age of sixty-five. Between 1954 and 1965 Hugh Wheeler published seven more Patrick Quentin novels, but in only one of them, *My Son, the Murderer* (1954) do the Duluths appear. This novel is narrated by Jake Duluth, a heretofore unknown brother of Peter Duluth, and details the extreme emotional travail he undergoes when his troubled son is implicated in a murder. Happily for Jake, Peter and Iris are on hand to extricate him from his troubles; by now the husband and wife were much seasoned experts in the field of foul play.

Peter Duluth takes his final bow in a Hugh Wheeler Patrick Quentin short story, "Death and the Rising Star" (also included in this volume), wherein Peter appropriately plays the lead role. Originally published in *Better Living Magazine* in 1955 and reprinted in *Ellery Queen's Mystery Magazine* in 1957, "Death and the Rising Star" takes Peter back to his position as a Broadway producer, involving him with a murder implicating an irrepressibly ambitious young actress named Didi Cheri. Throughout the story Wheeler amusingly name drops with abandon, mentioning such notable individuals as Danny Kaye, Marlene Dietrich, Tallulah Bankhead, Bernard Baruch, Greta Garbo, Averell Harriman, Claire Bloom and Clare Booth Luce.

After 1960 Hugh Wheeler became increasingly involved with writing for films and the stage, where he enjoyed distinguished success. Later in life he would win a trio of Tony awards, in recognition of the books he wrote for the musicals *A Little Night Music, Candide* and *Sweeney Todd*. Shortly after his death in 1987 at the age of seventy-five, most of the Patrick Quentin novels were reprinted by International Polygonics, Ltd. (IPL), a small press that will be fondly remembered by classic mystery aficionados who were around in those days. One of the reprinted mystery titles, *Puzzle for Players*, included an introduction by series consultant Douglas G. Greene, who was later to become the biographer of John Dickson Carr and the founder and owner of Crippen & Landru. In his introduction to *Players*, Greene noted that Rickie Webb and his partners in what might be termed the Q. Patrick/Patrick Quentin/Jonathan Stagge consortium "did not write books of the 'chess problem' sort in which the main interest lies in the cleverness of the solution....the question of 'whodunit' is not merely a game to puzzle a larger-than-life sleuth, but is an issue of life or death to the hero and heroine." In the Patrick Quentin Peter Duluth series in particular, Webb and Wheeler evolved from the comparatively traditional detective novels *Puzzle for Fools* and *Puzzle for Players* to the psychological suspense tales of the Forties and Fifties, thereby successfully navigating the curving course that mid-century American crime fiction followed in those years; yet always their plotting was clever and their characters credible and compelling, making the Peter Duluth mystery series a most impressive accomplishment indeed. Surely one of the greatest puzzles concerning Rickie Webb and Hugh Wheeler is how it is that in the country of their adoption their superlative crime fiction had almost entirely fallen out of print. With *The Puzzles of Peter Duluth,* Crippen & Landru once again has vindicated the reputation of an undeservedly neglected classic mystery writer and provided fans with yet another fine volume of vintage crime fiction.

Curtis Evans
thepassingtramp.blogspot.com

Death Rides the Ski-Tow

O it was one of those mean city February nights. Snow, which had been falling since sundown, was trying to make the Third Avenue El look quaint and amusing. It didn't succeed. I resented Third Avenue. I resented the snow sneaking down my neck and over the gunwales of my evening shoes. I resented it for being three o'clock in the morning. Particularly I resented Mrs. Ingoldsby for dragging her dinner party to Harlem to hear *but* the latest thing in boogie-woogie, and then snitching the only taxi and leaving me to fend for myself.

Not that I should have resented Mrs. Ingoldsby, since she was graciously backing my new production. But I did.

I was not strictly sober.

We had Third Avenue to ourselves, the snow and I. The drab uptown stores were shrouded in a dead darkness. Not a mouse stirring. I wished I was up skiing in New England, where there was some point to snow. A block ahead a single neon light gleamed forlornly over a hamburg joint. I made for it. Maybe I could telephone for a taxi. Maybe black coffee would make a little more dignified my homecoming to Iris, who had exercised her wifely prerogative and reneged on the party with an imaginary headache. Certainly there would be company.

You can get powerful lonely alone on a dark, late, empty New York night. Lonely—and scary. Anything might happen.

I was just starting down the block when the girl in the fur coat came out of the hamburg joint. She paused a moment under the neon sign, staring down Third Avenue away from me. Then she whipped around, saw me, and came running through the snow toward me. She came right up to me, standing squarely in front of me. She said desperately, "Please, please ..." And then her voice went away in a little whimper. It didn't make sense.

She was a blonde. Pretty, but had been prettier five years ago. The coat was mink. A scarf, covering her hair, was knotted under her chin. An evening gown showed under the coat. I wasn't too tight to see that there was terror in her eyes, real, mortal terror.

"You! Whoever you are. You've got to help me."

She glanced shudderingly over her shoulder. That was the first time I saw the car, saw its headlights creeping up Third Avenue toward us.

WITH A QUICK, convulsive gesture the girl pulled me into a dark doorway and thrust something into my hand. "You'll be paid anything you ask if you take this and ..." She pulled an envelope out of her pocket. "Take it and this letter to the address here on the envelope. Take it at once. Whatever happens ..."

She glanced out of the doorway, fear fluttering in her eyes like a bird. The car was closer, coming slowly, relentlessly, as if its driver were scanning every inch of the sidewalk for something or someone.

I took the letter stupidly. I stared at the other thing she had pressed into my hand. I knew then that I must be much, much drunker than I thought. Because the thing in my hand, wrapped in a paper napkin, was a hot dog. A mundane, five-cent frankfurter.

The drone of the car engine, crazily sinister, was the only sound in that drugged, snow-blanketed drab world.

"Here! Here are the keys to the apartment. George may not be home yet, and, if he isn't, wait there for him. Wait!" The girl pushed keys into my hand. "Tell him they know. Tell him they're out to get us. That there's danger, terrible danger. Tell ..."

The car was almost directly opposite us now. It slowed almost to a standstill. Suddenly a man's voice from inside called, "There she is!"

The girl stood there pressed against the wall by my side, shivering. Then the door of the car opened. She gave a wild little sob, broke away, dashed down the steps, and started running pointlessly off up Third Avenue. Like a hound dog unleashed, the car roared forward. She was running toward the corner, trying to get into the side street. The scarf over her head fluttered in the snow. She reached the hydrant, zigzagging. The car had passed me and was abreast of her. She looked at it wildly and screamed.

Then, with the scream, the sound of a shot barked. One shot and then another. The girl staggered sideways. Her arms were flung up over her head. She crumpled and fell, sprawling face downward in the snow. I could see her skirt, trailed over the snow—scarlet.

The car was still there, a gray, low-slung sedan. But I didn't think about it. You don't think about things at moments like that. I stuffed the hot dog, the keys, and the envelope in my overcoat pocket and started running forward toward the girl. It was madness, of course. I realized it just in time as the car ground into reverse and started backing.

"That guy was with her!"

I threw myself down on the snowy sidewalk only a split second before they fired at me. But I couldn't stay there flat on the sidewalk. I knew there was no safety there. I pushed myself up. Dodging, running doubled up, I sprinted toward a dark doorway. I leaped up the steps and pressed myself against the inside wall of the porch. A second bullet whistled past me splintering the glass in the front door behind me.

THEY WOULD HAVE got me if New York hadn't been New York. Already windows were springing into light across the street. I heard someone shouting and running. Fairly far away I heard a piercing police whistle. In those few seconds Third Avenue had come to life.

The car, that gray, low-slung sedan, paused murderously a moment, directly outside my doorway. I had a glimpse of two vague male faces inside. I couldn't see the number. Snow clogged it. Then, with a screeching of gears, it gathered speed and shot up Third Avenue—and away.

I was alone in the doorway. My heart was pounding. Under the street lamp at the corner, I could see the girl, sprawled there in the snow, a heap of scarlet and mink, small, pitiful, somehow unquestionably dead.

I started to the head of the steps to go to her. Then the people began to come. A woman with a man's camel's-hair overcoat over pajamas; a man, bald and bareheaded, wearing an apron; a workman in blue jeans; two little old people, clinging to each other—all of them converging on the corner, grouping around the girl, shouting, fussing.

If I hadn't been drinking I wouldn't have done what I did then. But suddenly, stupidly, I couldn't take it any more. Lurid visions rose up in my mind—visions of newspaper headlines: *Peter Duluth, well-known theatrical producer, involved in murder of girl on Third Avenue*; visions of Mrs. Ingoldsby whisking away her backing from my new show, visions of Iris suspicious, estranged, hurtling me into the divorce court.

All I wanted, in my shaken, befuddled state, was to get away, to pretend this crazy thing hadn't happened. So I didn't make a move. I waited there in the doorway, choosing my moment. Then I slipped down into the snow, heading away from that little excited cluster at the street corner.

I walked out on that poor, dead blonde....

GUILT ONLY CAME to me when I was safely out of the way in a bar on Lexington Avenue. Guilt and anger. Another, much-needed Scotch and soda had given me Dutch courage, and I felt bitter indignation against those unknown men in the gray sedan who had tried to kill me.

I felt sorry for the blonde, too, and ashamed of my desertion. I wanted to make amends. And there was an obvious way to make amends and also to avenge those bullets that had whizzed past my ear. The girl had been trying to get something through to someone called George, something important enough to the men in the gray sedan for them to have shot her dead. She'd given me all the stuff and she'd made a dying request. Okay. I'd take the message to George—whatever it involved.

I went into a booth, where I could be alone. I took the hot dog out of my pocket. There it was, a perfectly bona fide hot dog in a roll. That was too difficult for me. I stuffed it back and took out the letter.

It was a white, cheap envelope and written on it in a large, shaky hand, was:

Mr. George Anstey,
135A East 69th Street,
New York City.

That was George, then. And that was my destination. I turned the envelope over. It wasn't stuck down properly. I thought I had a right to open it. I did. There was a folded sheet of paper inside. I unfolded it and stared at it.

It said in five, concise words:

Nuts to you, Alessandro.
                    Hilda.

That helped a lot!

I folded the paper again and put it back in the envelope. I stuck the flap down the way it was supposed to be. I put the letter back in my pocket. For a moment I just stood there in the booth. Then I went through the bar to a phone and called Iris.

"Darling, I'm late."

"Yes, darling, you are."

"And I'm going to be later, because I've got a little errand to run for a friend."

"Blonde or brunette?" asked Iris.

"Blonde," I said. And then, trying to make it sound better: "She's dead."

I rang off. By a miracle I found a taxi. It took me to 135A East 69th Street.

I paid the taxi off and looked at the house. It was just an ordinary old brownstone house made over into apartments. Very run-of-the-mill. No lights showed in the windows. There wasn't a hall light, either. I took out the keys Hilda had given me. One for the outside door, one for the apartment door, presumably.

I walked up the steps. I looked around, but there was no one on the street. No gray, low-slung sedan.

I had to light a match to read the names on the buzzers. I saw, "GEORGE ANSTEY: APT. 4." I thought about ringing the buzzer, but decided against it. If the wrong person was in the apartment there was no point in heralding my approach.

One of the keys opened the front door. It was just light enough to see stairs stretching up. I found the banisters and, guiding myself, started as softly as I could up to Apartment 4. George had the penthouse apartment. I lit a match. I was in a small, dreary hallway. There was only one door. Before the match flickered out, I saw the card:

GEORGE ANSTEY

No light came out from under the door. I remembered how Hilda had said maybe George wouldn't be home yet. That made me less cautious as I struck another match and fumbled the second key into the lock. I made quite a racket.

The door opened inward onto darkness. I stepped across the threshold, and instantly a light was snapped on—not by me. I blinked at a rather meager living-room-office with a flat-topped desk and filing cabinets. Standing by the desk, a reading lamp at his side, was a very dark Latin young man with a swagger overcoat open at the front. There was snow on his shoulders that hadn't all melted, and he was covering me with a revolver gripped in a gloved hand.

I WISHED I hadn't come. Distinctly. As I stared at the revolver I tried to make my mind work. He had snow on his shoulders. That meant he had only just arrived. He hadn't taken off his coat. That meant he didn't live there. He was obviously South European. That meant his name probably wasn't George Anstey. He had been waiting in the dark with a revolver, waiting for someone to come. That meant ...

Alessandro, I thought. And I felt something prickling at the back of my neck.

He was glowering at me, surlily, arrogantly. "Who are you?" he said.

"Just a pal of George's." I tried to grin. "Good old George. Just dropped in for a quick one. Don't mind me."

"You came in wid a key." The revolver moved the fraction of an inch.

"A key? Oh, yes, sure. George gave me one. I'm from out of town. He lets me shake down here." And then, quite stupidly and drunkenly, I added, "I'm okay, Alessandro."

That was a fatal mistake. When I said his name he came at me with the revolver. We went into a clinch. More by luck than by judgment, I knocked the gun out of his hand. I made a lousy swing at his jaw, and missed. I hadn't a prayer then. I saw his face, very close and smiling a contented smile of anticipation. Then I felt his left gloved fist crash into my face....

I opened my eyes onto darkness. I was extremely sober, remembering every incident that had happened and regretting them all. I was lying on my back on the floor. I was gripping something in my right hand. I didn't pay it much attention. My nose was very painful. I raised my left hand to it gingerly. It wasn't broken, just swollen. I didn't feel very secure lying there in the dark. I pushed myself up, not letting go of whatever it was in my hand. Was I still in George Anstey's apartment or had they taken me somewhere else? I didn't even know that.

I stood still in the darkness, thinking of Alessandro. The pale pattern of the window gave me my bearings. I moved toward it, stumbling against furniture. If I was in Anstey's apartment, there had been a light on the desk and the desk had been by the window. I reached the window, my hands outstretched in front of me. My fingers felt the smooth surface of wood. The desk. I fumbled, found a light, and switched it on.

I stared at the thing in my hand. It was a heavy brass candlestick. It didn't mean anything to me—not at first. Then it meant a whale of a lot when I saw something dark and viscous on the end of it. Blood … !

I put it down quickly and looked around. I was in Anstey's apartment, all right. It was just the way it … I had to cling to the desk to steady myself. Very slowly, like a child-actor teaching itself lines, I made myself think, *"I am Peter Duluth, fairly well-known Broadway figure. This is New York City, New York State, U. S. A. Iris is at home waiting for me. Everything is going to be all right."*

That helped a bit, but not much.

Because, just inside the door, slumped over the worn, red carpet, was the body of a man I had never seen before. A thin, wiry man in a crumpled tuxedo, with yellowish hair and a pale, thin profile. There was red on his hair, red from a wound back of his left ear.

I STARED GLASSILY at him and then at the candlestick I had been holding. It wasn't hard to put one and one together. I could have wept. I went to the man, dropping on my knees at his side. I felt his pulse, did all these things. I knew they were useless, of course. You only had to look at him to realize he was dead.

Because I was reacting mechanically, I started running through his pockets for something that could identify him. It didn't take long. There was a bunch of cards in his wallet. They read:

GEORGE ANSTEY   HILDA PURVIS
Private Investigators

And then the address and telephone number.

So this was George Anstey. I thought of the blonde, who had once been prettier, stumbling through the snow, her scarf fluttering. Hilda Purvis.

This hadn't been a lucky night for George and Hilda. It wasn't lucky for me, either.

I hadn't the slightest idea what to do, because I was an averagely respectable citizen and nothing even remotely like this had ever happened to me before. All the time, my mind went on coping logically with the facts.

George Anstey must have come home while I was lying unconscious on the floor. Alessandro had been waiting behind the door with the candlestick. As Anstey let himself in, Alessandro had bopped him, and that had been curtains for George.

I started thinking how very close I had been to having the same thing happen to me. That knocked out what little control I had left. I had to get out of this place, quickly. I ran to the door, skirting Anstey's body. I turned the handle and pulled.

The door didn't move.

I tugged again wildly. Nothing happened. It had been bolted or somehow successfully jammed from the outside.

It's a singularly unattractive sensation being locked in a strange apartment with a strange corpse. I thought of my fingerprints on the candlestick and broke into a cold sweat. Maybe Alessandro wasn't so dumb, after all. He'd shut me in. My fingerprints were on the murder weapon; my fingerprints were on the body, all over the place. What if Alessandro had called the police from a phone booth? What if they arrived at any minute now? How could I explain my presence? How possibly could I make the police believe a story which even I, myself, hadn't really been able to believe yet?

IN A KIND of nervous crisis, I thought about smashing the door open and making my escape. But I didn't dare. Someone might hear. I couldn't risk being caught up with until I was a lot steadier.

I tried to think of it as a play, something impersonal in which I was only one of several actors. George Anstey and Hilda Purvis had been private investigators. Judging from the tacky apartment-office, they had been pretty small time, and, judging from the way Anstey looked, pretty shady, too. Probably playing a keyhole racket for the pickings. But this time, either working alone or hired by someone else, they'd obviously run up against something big—something involving my pal Alessandro and my other unknown pals in the gray, low-slung sedan.

That was clear enough. Just as it was clearer that Alessandro and his boy-friends had resented their meddling, to the extent of filling Hilda with lead and cracking George's skull with a candlestick.

But what of my role? Presumably tonight Hilda had stumbled upon some really vital information. She knew the gray sedan was after her and she couldn't get in touch with George. So she stopped the first sucker she ran up against on the street—which had been me—and had passed the buck on to him.

But what had the buck been? A letter to George and a hot dog. I'd read the letter, with its terse, derisive message to Alessandro. Surely it had contained no vital information. Unless it was in code. I felt in my overcoat pocket. I wanted to read the message through again.

The hot dog was still there in a mess of napkin and crumbled roll. But the letter had gone. Alessandro had taken it, of course. In spite of myself, my eyes shifted to George Anstey lying there unpleasantly dead in front of me. I felt rather sick.

Hilda got it all wrong. The note should have read, *Nuts to you, George and Hilda*. There might have been a P. S. about Peter Duluth, too.

IT SHOWS HOW dumb you can be if you try. It was only then, when the truth was screaming itself at me, that I thought of the hot dog. Beautiful women in mortal terror of death, don't press hot dogs into the hands of strangers without a purpose.

Feverishly I pulled the hot dog, with its broken wrapping of roll, out of my pocket. I took the frankfurter between finger and thumb. It had been boiled, not split and fried. I turned it around. I saw what I should have seen from the start—a small, uneven slit in the skin. And, just visible sticking out of it, a tiny piece of paper.

I pulled the paper out. Clearly visible in small, penciled writing, were the words:

SWITCHED FROM SKI-FLYER N. H. TO SKI-MONARCH VT. 8:30 TOMORROW GRAND CENTRAL. TRANSFER 10 A. M. NORTHERN FOOT OF RAMP.

That cryptic message meant nothing to me. I had no idea what had been switched from the Ski-Flyer to the Ski-Monarch ski-train nor what transfer was going to take place at the northern foot of what ramp. But I thought I saw exactly what had been in Hilda's mind when she stopped me on the street. And my sympathy for her sorry fate dwindled considerably.

Hilda must have known there was a good chance that Alessandro would be waiting in Anstey's apartment. She was desperately keen for Anstey to get the dope about the ski-train, but she was equally keen to save his life. She knew he might be out. So she gave me keys to the apartment, the phony note, and the hot dog. I was to have been the sacrificial goat. My function had been to arrive at the apartment before Anstey returned, open the door with the key as only the owner would do, and be bopped over the head in mistake for George. Alessandro, discovering he had killed the wrong man, wouldn't have dared hang around with a corpse waiting for Anstey. He would have decamped, waiting only to search me. The letter would have deflected him from the hot dog. He would have dashed off thinking he'd got the information. *Nuts to you, Alessandro.* Very apt.

Later George would have arrived home unmolested. True, it would have been uncomfortable to find a corpse in his apartment, but less uncomfortable than being the corpse himself. And, since Hilda and George had probably used the hot dog as a carrier pigeon before, he would have got the information, too.

Very smart of Hilda. I shuddered when I thought how nearly her plan had succeeded.

I stared down again at the note. The ramp meant nothing. A ramp in Grand Central? But the Ski-Monarch meant a lot. Iris and I, who were crazy about skiing, had taken it last year. A very deluxe trip to Greenfield, Vermont, almost on the Canadian border, where two days were spent at the swanky Mountain Inn at the foot of the celebrated Hurricane Trail.

How on earth was the Ski-Monarch mixed up with this? I couldn't tell, of course.

Instinctively, because I had read detective stories and was clue-conscious, I slipped the message back into the frankfurter, wrapped the whole thing in a piece of paper, and put it into my pocket. One didn't destroy clues. Exhibit A, I thought.

And now that I knew more or less what I was up against I felt a lot better. Better and mad—mad with Hilda, George, Alessandro, and the whole gang. If they thought they could do this to me, a harmless, law-abiding citizen, they were crazy.

There was a telephone on the desk. I would call the police. Yes. Why not? I was innocent. I had nothing to fear.

I looked at Anstey's body lying there on the red carpet. Suddenly, calling the police didn't seem such a good idea, after all.

And then, just as I was thinking about the phone, it started to ring. It was a thin, horrible sound in that silent room. *Pin-n-n-n-ng ... pin-n-n-n-ng ...* I stood staring at it, stifling a painless impulse to flight.

THE PHONE RANG on. Slowly my hand went out. Then the nerve-racking thought came: "Maybe it's Alessandro to find out if I'm still here." Should I? Shouldn't I? ... I did. I picked up the receiver.

Of course, I didn't know how George talked. But most men, I figured, talked the same sort of way when they'd been awakened at four o'clock. I mumbled, "'Ullo."

A woman's voice, one of the throaty, glamour variety which comes sixteen to the dozen in show-business, said urgently, "George, this is Juliana. Is Hilda back yet?"

I thought of Hilda lying on the street corner huddled in the snow. Simply and truthfully I said, "No."

"George, I'm worried, are you?"

Once again, very truthfully, I said, "Yes."

"George, I'm calling about my pocket-book. I just realized I must have left it at your house this evening. A white one. I'm sure I left it in the bedroom when I fixed my hair. Be a darling and see if it's there."

I found myself staring straight at George's dead left foot. I flicked my eyes away. "'Kay, Juliana. Hold on."

I hurried to the door of the inner room and turned on a wall switch. It was a bedroom, all right, with twin beds. On a repulsive mahogany bureau I saw a woman's white evening bag. I was about to go back to the phone when I noticed, jubilantly, that there was an iron fire escape right outside the bedroom window. I'd never thought about a fire escape. Exit had been as elementary as all that!

I took up the receiver again. "Sure, Juliana; it's there."

"What a relief!" Juliana throbbed. "George, will you be an angel and bring it around right away? The tickets are in it."

"Okay. I'll bring it around."

"Angel! And don't worry about the money. You'll get it as soon as Hilda crashes through. I'll be seeing you, then."

"Sure. But hold on, Juliana. Wha'—wha's the address?"

"But, George, you *know* the address.

"Kind of sleepy. 'S gone out of my mind."

"Silly!" Juliana laughed exotically, gave a number on Park Avenue, and rang up.

I didn't know what I'd got myself into now. I didn't really care much. The discovery of the fire escape had given me a kind of devil-may-care assurance. I went into the bedroom and brought the pocketbook back to the desk. I opened it.

In a little pocket in the lining was a small envelope. Inside it were tickets. I took them out. Two train tickets with two accompanying drawing-room stubs. On the stubs I read: "Ski-Flyer, Franconia, N. H."

The Ski-Flyer! The wrong ski-train.

I remembered: *"You'll get the money when Hilda crashes through."* I fingered the frankfurter in my pocket. Then I had been right. George and Hilda had been working for someone higher up. And that someone higher up was the glamorous, larynxed Juliana.

Just at that particular moment there was a distinct rap on the door. I looked at Anstey's body. I felt my pulses drumming like Meade Lux Lewis's boogie-woogie.

The rapping came again. Louder. More authoritative. And a harsh, male voice said, "Open up in the name of the law."

The police! Feverishly I tugged out a handkerchief and wiped my fingerprints off the candlestick. But what good did that do? My fingerprints were on the desk, the telephone, the light switch, the … And, adding the last excruciating touch, the hideous recollection came that last week, at Mrs. Ingoldsby's patriotic suggestion, I had submitted my fingerprints to the city in the mayor's Good Citizenship drive.

Good Citizenship!

THE RAPPING ON the door was very insistent now. "Open up—or we'll bash the door in!"

How could I possibly explain my behavior to the police now? I couldn't. I grabbed up Juliana's pocketbook. My heart racing, I tiptoed to the bedroom, eased up the window, slipped out onto the platform of the fire escape, and lowered the window cautiously behind me.

I reached ground level. I was in a kind of yard at the back of the apartment house. It was surrounded on three sides by a high, distinctly unscalable wall. I ran through the snow to the wall parallel to the house. There must be a door.

There was. But it was clamped shut by a large padlock.

I turned back to the house itself. I had no choice. There were steps going down to a wooden door, presumably leading to a cellar. I groped my way down them to the door. It wasn't locked. I pushed it open and stole inside, into cavernous darkness.

I lit a match, and its feeble flame revealed a regular cellar. I could see a furnace. The air was pungent with coal-gas fumes. My only hope was that the cellar stretched all the way under the house and had an exit onto 69th Street. It was hardly the ideal route, because it would bring me smack out under the nose of the police car. But that was a risk which had to be run.

Lighting match after match, I crept on. At last I made out a door ahead. Above it was a square skylight. That meant I was below street level. That was something.

I went to the door. My hand hit a padlock like the one on the yard door. Then, an exquisite relief, my fingers felt a key. I unlocked the padlock. Shakily I opened the door inward. Snow scattered in and with it the pale light from the street.

I slipped out. I was in a little areaway. Iron railings above marked the street. There was a flight of stone steps leading up.

Vaguely I had expected sound, excitement. Didn't that always happen when the police arrived? But there was no sound.

GINGERLY I STARTED up the snowy steps. Six steps up I stopped, because my eyes were then at street level. It was a rather crazy sensation having my eyes on the sidewalk. A cat's view of New York.

I looked for the police car, parked outside 135A. It was on the other side of the street about fifty feet away. And I recognized it as definitely as I could ever recognize any car. It wasn't a police car. It was the gray, low-slung sedan.

I stood there halfway up the steps, feeling a cold chill which was half fear, half fury. Then I heard muffled footsteps echoing on the sidewalk, and I ducked down into the areaway, pressing myself against the wall in the shadow.

The person who was walking toward 135A was coming fast. The footsteps grew nearer and nearer. From where I stood in the shadow I would be able to get a good view without being seen, myself. In a few seconds the pedestrian came into my sphere of vision. I saw him in a queer, low-angle way. But that was all I needed. It wasn't difficult to recognize my buddy, Alessandro.

He hurried past me, almost at a run, and swerved up the front steps of 135A. I heard the door open and close softly behind him. It was obvious what had happened upstairs now. Alessandro must have telephoned an account of his exploits to the two unknown men of the gray sedan and they had returned, probably to finish off his halfhearted job. Alessandro, presumably, had the only keys and he had been late for the party. So they had pretended to be the police, in the hope of tricking me into letting them in.

When they found me gone they were bound to come down right away.

I didn't have to wait long. Scarcely five minutes after Alessandro's hurried entrance into 135A, I heard indeterminate sounds, sounds that became footsteps, the opening of a door, and then low voices. I couldn't see the men. They were standing inside the dark outer hallway of the house, almost immediately above my head. But I heard Alessandro's voice, blustering, self-vindicating:

"... You didn't tell me nuttin' about this guy, Steve. You just say over the phone to get Anstey; then this guy comes in, acts phony, and so I sock him. Then, after Anstey got back and I fixed him, this guy's still there out cold on the floor — see? I figure maybe you'd wanna give him a once-over, so I lock him in. And I stick the candlestick in his hand, so's if the cops get there first, then they'd figure he slugged Anstey."

"Even though he was lying unconscious on the floor and locked into the apartment from the outside! Very brilliant, Alessandro." This second voice, presumably "Steve's," was soft, with a queer lilt to it which wasn't exactly American and yet not exactly foreign, either. "And you saved him for me by leaving him there with a perfectly good fire escape. In the immortal words of Hilda Purvis: *Nuts to you, Alessandro.*"

That was the flossiest speech I'd ever heard from a crook. But, even so, that soft voice did something to the back of my neck. It was as ruthless and velvet-glove an affair as I'd hope to run up against, on stage or off.

"So you let him get away. The man who was with Hilda tonight on Third Avenue, the man who's almost certainly the one they sold us out to, the only person who could wreck our whole plan. We don't even know his name."

"Ain't got his name?" Alessandro's snort was outraged. "What you t'ink I am? Course I frisked him for a gat. And I found a card. It's got his name on. Peter Duluth. And a coupla addresses where he lives."

"Peter Duluth, eh? I believe there's a theatrical producer of that name. I wonder ... Show me the card, Alessandro."

I felt as if I'd swallowed a cupful of cold oatmeal.

"Yes," said Steve's voice. "So that's the man. Maybe you have redeemed yourself a little, Alessandro."

A third voice spoke for the first time; it was young and anxious: "Listen, Steve; we better get out of here. For all you know, this Duluth guy called the police."

"Unless I'm very much mistaken, Dickie, Mr. Duluth will steer as clear of the police as we do. He'll be playing a lone hand now. Well, we know his address. There should be plenty of time to make his acquaintance before eight-thirty tonight."

8:30. That was the time the Ski-Monarch left Grand Central.

Plenty of time to make his acquaintance.... Those words, so assured, so silky smooth, so unnerving, rang in my ears as feet shuffled down the snowy steps above me.

THEN STEVE'S VOICE said, "Wait," and the man in the middle stooped down to tie his shoelace. I couldn't see his face because his hat was pulled down. But, as his right hand stretched out of his sleeve over the shoe, the light from the cigarette in his mouth lit up the skin above his wrist. And, distinctly, I saw there a blue, thin scar, shaped like a half-moon.

It was all over in a second. Steve stood up again and they moved on. But, just as they had almost passed out of sight, he reached across Alessandro and flicked the cigarette stub into the basement.

It dropped almost at my feet. And it seemed to me that suddenly there was a faint, sweet smell in the cold February air. I picked up the stub. I sniffed it. Yes, there was a definite perfume. I shifted from the shadows to the middle of the areaway, where dim light struck down from the street light. The cigarette had a gold tip and, written in small gold letters across the white paper, was the word: *Fortuna.*

That voice, that scar, that brand of cigarettes. At least I had something to recognize Steve by, when we met again.

I heard the gray sedan start in the street above me. For a minute or so after the sound of it had faded into the distant noises of pre-dawn New York, I stayed there in the areaway. I faced my predicament squarely for the first time. There was no longer anything gay or debonair about it. My fingerprints in the murder-apartment—thanks to Mrs. Ingoldsby and the mayor—were bound to involve me hopelessly with the police. Alessandro's sinister, soft-spoken boss not only knew my name, he assumed that I was the person who had bribed Anstey into double-crossing him, the person who was out to frustrate his mysterious expedition on the Ski-Monarch. For that, if for nothing else, he would certainly stop at nothing to send me after George and Hilda.

I felt frightened and strangely self-assured at the same time. I weighed my assets. Juliana, obviously, was the foremost. Juliana, with the glamour voice and the two tickets for the wrong ski-train; Juliana, who was sitting at home in Park Avenue waiting for her bag, waiting for Hilda to "crash through." Over the phone I had promised to take her pocketbook back to her. I hadn't really meant it then. But things were very different now. Everything seemed to point my next move distinctly toward Juliana.

JULIANA'S PARK AVENUE apartment house managed to exude class even at that hour of the morning. Although there was nothing I could do about my swollen nose, I made the rest of myself as respectable as possible and pushed through glass doors into a fancy, lighted vestibule. A bored colored night porter and an even more bored redhead behind the switchboard stared at me. It was only then that the uncomfortable realization came that I didn't know whom to ask for. Juliana. Just plain Juliana. There seemed only one thing to do.

I became suddenly drunk. I reeled to the desk. I fixed the redhead with what was probably a genuinely bleary eye and muttered thickly, "Mis-sh Juliana ...," then a series of completely indistinguishable syllables which, I hoped, would cover any name from Levy to Buttersthwaite.

Rather to my surprise it worked like a charm. The redhead stared gloomily and said, "Whooshllizayzcalling?"

"George Anstey."

That had been risky, but the girl showed no skepticism.

She said down a mouthpiece, "Mr. Anstey here." And then, "Okay." She glared at the porter over my shoulder. "Take him up to 12, Humbolt."

Humbolt did.

"Second door to the right," he said, and slammed the elevator gates behind me.

I was in a very voguish hallway with frameless mirrors and mole-gray rugs. I might have felt apprehensive of danger. But I didn't. I counted doors. Second to the right. I reached it. There was a stylish card inserted in the door. I leaned forward to read it, but, before I could do so, the door was opened inward and a girl trailing clouds of exotic negligee swirled out.

"George, you're an ange—" she began, and then stopped dead, staring at me.

I was staring at her, too. It was a most awkward moment for both of us. I stammered, "Julie."

And she stammered, "Peter."

And I was thinking, Juliana Guilder. Of course. Why in heaven's name hadn't I recognized that voice over the phone? That all goes to show how passion dies.

Four years ago Juliana Guilder, The Dutch Tulip, Broadway's most publicized glamour actress, had been, voice and all, the most torrid thing in my life. Three years ago she had been the most glacial thing in my life. One year ago, when I met Iris, Juliana had become something infinitely embarrassing and to be avoided, who found me equally embarrassing and to be avoided.

Juliana was the one person in New York I liked the idea of seeing least. Now—here she was.

After the first second of shock Julie gathered her face together, and it was one of the most sensational faces ever to have immigrated from Amsterdam, Holland. "Peter, so you've come to see me. How charming! But I was expecting someone quite ..." Then her eyes, behind their lustrous lashes, fell on her pocketbook under my arm. That stopped that. She looked blank and then almost crafty, and said, "Come in, Peter."

SHE TOOK MY hand and drew me into the apartment, shutting the door behind us. She led the way, using her body for all it was worth. And it was worth a lot. It was the chic apartment to end all chic apartments. Plate glass, pastels, and Picassos. Far more expensively chic, I reflected cynically, than even Juliana could swing without assistance.

She lounged onto a couch and patted the cushion next to her. In the old days that would have excited me. Even at five o'clock in the morning. Now I was far more interested in something I saw in the corner:

Two pairs of skis, neatly bound together with their accompanying ski poles. And, under them, the very latest thing in Norwegian leather rucksacks.

Two lots of skis. Two tickets for the Ski-Flyer. Juliana. And who else?

Abandoning the almost automatic seduction act, Juliana said rather shrilly, "George Anstey was going to bring my bag back. At the desk you said you were George Anstey."

I had to walk very warily. Juliana was nobody's fool. I took the handbag from under my arm and handed it to her. Why not? I said, "I happened to be around at George's and he asked me to bring it for you. I gave his name downstairs. Less complicated."

She stared at me doubtfully. "Did he send a message?"

"Just to make sure about the money when Hilda crashes through."

She blurted, "And has Hilda crashed through?"

I put my hand in my overcoat pocket and touched the frankfurter which, on account of that scrap of paper inside it, had cost Hilda her life. Poor Hilda! "Sure," I said. "Hilda crashed through."

Juliana's eyes flashed. "Then tell me. What ... ?" She broke off, as if she realized she'd made a mistake. "But you're not working with George and Hilda. You can't be. And when I called I woke him up. He'd been asleep—alone."

"Sure. I just happened to drop in later, after you'd called."

She was really suspicious now. "I don't believe you. This is a trap. Why—why did you go to see George?"

I tried shifting my ground. "Oh, I'd just been out with the boys."

"The boys?"

That seemed the moment for the *blitzkrieg*. "Yes," I said. "The boys. Alessandro and Steve and ..."

"Steve!" The complexion which had put Holland in soap ads from coast to coast turned faintly green. "Stephen Dorn," she whispered. "You were with Stephen Dorn!"

The *blitzkrieg* had worked. I knew my antagonist's full name now: Stephen Dorn. A big step in the right direction.

"Yes," I said. "Alessandro, Stephen Dorn, and" — remembering the name Steve had used for the third man — "Dickie."

She did stand up then. For a moment I thought she was going to faint. She came to me, all chiffon and Chanel. She gripped my arm. "Stephen Dorn sent you here!" she babbled. "He knows about us. He's found out that George and Hilda double-crossed him for us, that we're after him. This is his way of showing he knows — sending you here. This ..."

If she went on that way much longer, she'd collapse. I saw I was defeating my own ends getting her that scared. So I shifted tactics again to try to quiet her. I said, "Stephen Dorn didn't send me here. He doesn't know there's a tie-up between you and Anstey." All of which was true. "And I never said I was working with Dorn, either. I'm not."

That worked like a miracle. Juliana was calm.

"Then who ...?" she began.

At that particular moment I heard the front door open and close. Juliana broke away from me and swirled around to face the hallway. I turned, ill-prepared for almost anything.

And then a man came in. A dark, smooth, expensive, middle-aged man with a little mustache and a thousand-dollar mink-lined overcoat. I recognized him — just the way everyone on Broadway would have recognized him. Derek Huysmans, the fabulously rich New York–Amsterdam diamond magnate who was the most sought-after play backer in show-business, the star angel of every producer's prayers.

So this, I reflected, was where the extra rental came from. This, too, was probably the other half of Julie's "us," her companion-to-be on the Ski-Flyer.

I LEFT THE social amenities to Juliana. She didn't do a very good job with them. With a kind of wild politeness she said, "Derek, this is Peter Duluth, the producer."

Derek Huysmans stared at me, or rather through me. He didn't seem surprised or jealous to find me there at five o'clock in the morning. He didn't even seem interested.

Juliana stopped trying to be poised. Distractedly she poured out to him every word I'd said. He was interested then. He swung round to me, very intent and poker-faced. "You've just come back from Anstey's, Mr. Duluth. Then you can possibly confirm something I've just heard over the radio. I've just heard that Hilda Purvis and Anstey have been murdered. Hilda was shot on a street corner. Anstey was killed in his apartment about three o'clock tonight."

That wasn't one of my best moments.

"Murdered!" echoed Juliana. "So—so Dorn found out. He got them." Slowly, very slowly, she turned to me. She stared at me as if I were something horrible and unclean. "You! When I called, George was dead. That voice on the phone, it was—you!"

They were both staring at me. I saw the ivory telephone on a glass table. I thought of the police. I felt sweat trickling down inside my undershirt.

Slowly, because it seemed the only possible thing to do, I started backing toward the door. My hand was still in my overcoat pocket. My fingers closed around Hilda's frankfurter and I pushed it forward, trying to make them think it was a gun. Probably it was a very feeble pretense. I didn't know. I wasn't used to scenes like that. I hadn't the ganster technique.

AS I BACKED to the door, neither of them tried to stop me. That gave me courage. Helped me to think, too. I said,

"Before you call the police, Juliana, you might remember that you were at Anstey's tonight yourself. It might be very ..."

"No one's going to call the police, Mr. Duluth." Huysmans was still watching me. Very calmly he moved to a desk, opened a drawer, and brought out a revolver. "And, since I rather doubt whether that is a gun in your pocket, perhaps you'd sit down and we can have a little talk."

I sat down, and he came closer, Juliana hovering at his side. "You told Juliana that you weren't one of Dorn's associates. Is that true?"

"Absolutely true." If I'd pretended to be tied up with Dorn, I was pretty sure Huysmans would have killed me then, neatly, and rung for a Japanese butler to remove the corpse. I added, with strict candor: "I'm just in this thing on my own."

"In that case I'd advise you very strongly to get out of it while you're still alive."

That wasn't designed to make me feel any better. "I can't get out of it—not until I've found out a few things. Why you and Juliana are going on the Ski-Flyer tomorrow, for example."

Huysmans's eyes flickered. Juliana said sharply, "He doesn't know anything, Derek. He just saw the tickets in my bag. It's a bluff."

"Is it also a bluff if I tell you that you're wasting your time going on the Ski-Flyer?" I asked.

That got them both. Huysmans stiffened. Juliana grabbed at his arm. "He talked about Hilda crashing through. Maybe he does know. Maybe ..."

Huysmans put the gun back in his pocket. He was very sure of himself. "I was planning to pay Anstey and Hilda Purvis a certain sum of money for certain information. If you have that information, Mr. Duluth, I am willing to pay you what I would have paid them."

"I'm not interested in money," I said. "I'm—Hell! I just want to know what it's all about."

Huysmans's face was as wooden as ever. He took the gun out of his pocket again. "Haven't you rather failed to grasp the situation, Mr. Duluth? I have a gun. You have certain information. Perhaps you would be good enough to give it to me."

Being killed by Huysmans would feel much the same as being killed by Dorn. I didn't give much of a darn, anyway. Why shouldn't he have his information? My hand went into my pocket. Suddenly it all seemed funny, deliriously, insanely funny. I took the frankfurter out of my pocket and handed it to him.

He snatched it eagerly, stripped off the wrapping, twisted it around, and pulled the little scrap of paper out of the slit in the skin. Juliana ran to his side, trailing chiffon, staring over his shoulder. Slowly they both looked up. There was an expression of triumph on their faces, real, honest-to-goodness triumph.

Huysmans went back to the desk, took out a checkbook, and scribbled. He came to me. "However you came by this information, Mr. Duluth, you deserve to be paid for it. And just one word of advice: Let this be the end of your interest in the affair. It will be considerably safer for you."

He pressed a check into my hand. I took it. I don't really know why. Largely, I suppose, because when people press checks into your hand you just naturally don't let go. I looked down at it. I felt a little dizzy. It was made out to me. And it was for $10,000.

As I moved dazedly to the door, Huysmans was still holding the frankfurter caressingly, as if it were a pearl of great price. Which, of course, it was. Probably the first $10,000 hot dog in the history of meat packing....

IT WAS STILL snowing when I left the apartment house. It was still dark, too. February nights seem to go on indefinitely. The check in my pocket still had me slightly giddy.

I knew a bit more of the picture now. Stephen Dorn was working some big deal, something concerned with skiing.

It had been fixed for the Ski-Flyer and New Hampshire, and then switched to the Ski-Monarch and Greenfield, Vermont. Greenfield was near the Canadian border. Was that it? Smuggling, perhaps? Something big, anyway; something big enough for Huysmans to have paid $10,000 for a hot-dogful of information about it.

I knew all that. Yes. But it didn't help me. I was still a fugitive from the police, from Dorn—from half of New York.

I scanned Park Avenue uneasily. There was no sign of the gray, low-slung sedan. But there was a taxi. I got it and gave my home address. The prospect of Iris was something very specially nice. Iris was so beautiful, so intelligent, so sane. Things would seem less unspeakable when I saw her.

We had almost reached the street I lived on when I came to my senses with a bang. Stephen Dorn had my address. For all I knew, the gray sedan was already waiting there outside the front door. I leaned forward shakily. I said to the driver, "Not the front door. Don't go down the front street. There's a service entrance at the back." I gave directions.

It went through without a hitch. There was nothing sinister about the service entrance, only a sleepy night watchman who took me up to my floor in the service elevator. I went to my own door. My heart started fluttering. It always does at the thought of seeing Iris. I took out my key. I let myself in.

The lights were on in the living-room. The heavy drapes were pulled. Iris was lying on the sofa in pajamas, her black hair rumpled over a cushion. You ought to see Iris asleep. It's one of the best things the human race has thought up— so serene, so beautiful, and yet so sensible, too.

She woke before I reached her. She got up, throwing back her hair and looking very young and unyielding. "Home is the scalp-hunter," she said nastily.

I went to her and took her in my arms and kissed her. "Iris!" Her hair smells so subtle. And the feel of her in your arms! Everything was so very all right again.

But I was still on the job. I went away from her. I turned out the light. I moved to the curtained window and pulled back the edge of the heavy drape. I had a direct view of the street below. I could see anything that was there to the end of the block.

I saw dark houses; I saw snowy, empty sidewalks; I saw the snow swirling down. And—I couldn't bear it. I just couldn't bear it—I saw, easing up to park at the curb on the other side of the street, a gray, low-slung sedan.

I let the curtain drop. I turned back to Iris. I said, "I shouldn't have come back. They're here. I shouldn't have come back. Now there'll be danger for you, too."

"What danger?"

"Just danger. Straight, simple danger. Darling, I've seen two murders tonight. I've been shot at. I've been locked up with a corpse. I've been given a check for ten thousand dollars. I've been chased by crooks in a car. They've just caught up with me again. They're outside."

I took her arms, just because I had to have some kind of contact with her. I told her everything from the very beginning.

She wasn't believing me. Gradually I came to realize that. She just thought I was drunk, and she was humoring me along.

"But it's true, darling. I can show you the check. And—look. Go to the window. Be careful, but look out. You'll see the car."

That was when the phone rang. I looked at Iris. She looked at me. I started for the phone; then, like lightning, she pushed ahead of me and took it. Her voice was perfect, the voice of the bewildered, injured wife. "No, Mr. Duluth isn't here.... Yes. He called about twenty minutes ago from the Pennsylvania Station. He said he was leaving for Washington right away.... It's all very sudden. I knew nothing about it. He didn't even come home and pack. Urgent business, he said. And he wouldn't be back for several days.... What? ... Yes. He said I could get in touch with him at the Sherry-Carlton. I'm sure you'll reach him there."

IRIS PUT DOWN the receiver. We looked at each other. Very quietly she said, "Okay, Peter. You win."

"The voice?"

"The most loathsome voice I ever heard—soft, cultured."

"Stephen Dorn."

"He said he was an actor who had an appointment with you in the morning. He apologized for calling at this hour, some reason he gave. It was perfectly plausible." Her voice had a funny little quiver in it. "Thank heaven, you were back in time to warn me. If he'd called five minutes earlier I wouldn't have suspected a thing. I'd have told him I was expecting you any moment."

She came to me then, slipping her hand in mine. "Peter, was I convincing? I wanted to fool him into thinking you'd got scared and cleared out. Do you think he believed me? Do you think he'll go away?"

"If they do, darling, you probably saved my life—for the time being, at least."

We went to the window and pulled back the drape just enough to see the gray sedan move swiftly away.

"We can turn the light on now." Iris's voice was cold, almost prim. She went from me and turned on a reading lamp. "Come sit on the couch."

I did.

"Now tell it to me all over again."

When it was all over, she said, "Peter, at the beginning, when the girl was shot, why didn't you wait there and tell the police everything when they came?"

I felt guilty. "I—I thought of the scandal. You know how Mrs. Ingoldsby ..."

"There needn't have been any scandal if you told the truth then. You must have known that."

I FELT EVEN guiltier. "Well, darling, you see I was kind of muddled. I'd been drinking and ..."

"That's more like it." She sat there looking utterly beautiful and as cool now as the Holland Tunnel. "Since you registered only last week in the Good Citizenship Drive, your fingerprints probably aren't filed in Washington yet. But they will be soon, and then the police will trace you."

"Exactly."

"And what are you going to tell them? How are you going to explain all the crazy things you've done?"

"I don't see how I can."

"Neither do I. Even if you wriggle out of a murder charge, you'll still be an accessory after the fact."

I thought of that—gloomily.

Suddenly, accusingly, Iris added, "You never told me you knew Juliana Guilder before we were married."

I faltered under that unexpected flank attack. I stammered, "Didn't I?—I guess I didn't think it would interest you."

"It was just a brief and beautiful friendship, I suppose. Quiet evenings together nodding over your needlepoint." She lapsed into momentary silence. Somehow I took it for granted she was going to make it all right. She looked as if an idea was coming. It came: "If Dorn believed me, he'll send someone to Washington after you. He'll surely send Alessandro, since he's the one who knows what you look like. That means the other two—Dorn and Dickie—won't have any way of recognizing you."

I said, with a certain sour dignity, "You forget that I'm a prominent man of the theater. My picture appears regularly in the newspapers."

"Publicity pictures!" said Iris. "Pooh!" She was becoming excited. She ran to a desk and came back with a big portfolio, untying ribbons. "I've kept them all. Look!" She strewed glossy portraits all over me, pointing derisively. "Look! Beautiful sheeny hair, lustrous eyes, Colman mustache, Barrymore nose. Who's going to recognize you from them?"

I bridled. I'd always thought those pictures were pretty good likenesses.

Iris was staring at me now with a kind of gimlet-eyed intentness. "Particularly with that nose, darling. It's amazing what Alessandro did. He's swelled it and flattened it. I don't know how long it will last, but it's too fascinatingly mulatto."

She came to me, throwing back her dark hair, sitting on the publicity photographs, taking my hands. "Yes, darling. That's it, of course. You better get some sleep, because we're going on the Ski-Monarch tonight."

I stared at her.

"It's perfect skiing weather, and I've been dying for weeks to try the Hurricane Trail again. Next week we'll be in production, and there won't be another chance this year."

"But, Iris ..."

"Don't you see how it's the only way?" She turned to me almost fiercely. "It's all coming to a head in Greenfield, isn't it? You're doomed if you just sit around here waiting for the police or Dorn to catch up with you. But if we go up there, find out what this fantastic thing is all about, and somehow get evidence, then we can go to the police with the whole story. They'll have to believe us then. And it'll only be then, when this Stephen Dorn and his friends are arrested, that there'll be any kind of safety for you."

That made crazy Iris-sort of sense.

"But Juliana and Huysmans will be on the train, too."

A contemptuous gesture swept them away. "They're as scared of Dorn as we are. We can keep an eye on them, and, with any luck, they'll give us a lead."

That made crazy Iris-sense, too.

"All right," I said bleakly. "I guess I've dug my grave, and I'll lie in it. But I'm not going to let you fool around with any Mata Hari act."

"Nonsense." Iris's eyes were gleaming. "Wild horses wouldn't keep me away." She paused. "On second thoughts, we'd better not travel together. Juliana doesn't know me, and I don't want her or anyone else to tab me as your wife. I can be much more use if I'm just a girl on her own." Her smile was rather unfriendly. "Maybe I'll find a masculine Juliana. Maybe I'll be picked up by a lovely ski-instructor with muscles."

Iris looked dreamy. A pause, and then, "One thing more, Peter."

"What, darling?"

"The check, darling. Hand it over."

I gave it to her. Firmly, severely, she tore it into little pieces. "No hot dog," she said, "is worth ten thousand bucks. We Duluths don't go in for that easy money."

And that was that....

MY NOSE WAS painful, but Iris refused to do anything about it. She was afraid the camouflage swelling would go down. At her insistence, I went sullenly to bed. Against all reason, I slept.

Iris came in, very gay, in an oyster-white negligee. She was carrying a cup of coffee. "So you're awake."

She sat down on the bed. She looked superb but executive. I pushed myself up and kissed her.

"Everything's arranged." She was taking it all as lightly as if it were a taffy-pull. "I've waxed the skis. And I've got the sleeper tickets. Yours is in your wallet. You're in R. 18. I'm in S. 37. I've decided that your name's Martin Jones. Mine's Cynthia Rowley." She looked romantic. "Isn't that a beautiful name, Peter?"

"A name to launch a thousand ski-instructors. Go on."

"The police haven't arrived. And there's been no sign of the gray sedan. But I'm taking no chances. I'll leave by taxi from the front. You'll wait ten minutes, and then leave in a taxi from the service entrance."

Suddenly I was hating it.

"On the Ski-Monarch we'll have absolutely nothing to do with each other. And it's your job to identify Dorn and Dickie without their recognizing you."

"Pick them out of two hundred and fifty unknown skiers?"

"Yes. And when we get to the Mountain Inn we watch— and foil."

"What could be simpler?" I groaned.

She got up and went out of the room. She came back with something small and black and gleaming. She held it out to me. "I got this for you."

"A revolver!"

"Well, it's only a prop revolver. I got it from Eddie at the Vandolan Theater. But it's the best I could do."

I took it. "Chasing unknown murderers with a toy revolver! Iris, we can't do it. It's too whimsical."

Iris looked very severe. "You'd rather be whimsical, wouldn't you—than dead?" ...

MY TAXI TOOK me through the snowy streets and dumped me at Grand Central Station. Iris had left the apartment ten minutes before me. Everything had run according to schedule. Having slept through the daylight hours, I had lost all sense of everything except darkness. This still seemed the same interminable night which had begun with Hilda Purvis sprawling dead in the snow. And my reaction to it was much the same.

But there's something exhilarating about the feel of skis on your shoulder. Something indestructibly unsinister about a modern railroad station. Brushing redcaps aside, I started down the ramp into the vast, animated arena. I wasn't Peter Duluth any more, I told myself. I was—whoosit?—Martin Jones, an enthusiastic, solitary skier bound for Vermont with his head full of stem-Christies and Telemarks.

I thought of Juliana and Huysmans. Would they be on the train yet? But even that couldn't change my holiday mood. I knew none of these healthy, ruddy-cheeked people. And surely none of them knew me. Surely it wasn't possible that hidden in all these innocent good spirits there lurked the unpleasant shadow of Stephen Dorn.

The Ski-Monarch, long, low, and green, stretched along the platform. With its lighted windows and grinning porters calling their Pullman numbers, it, too, seemed to have a sportive, vacation air.

And then, suddenly, as I moved along in the crowd, I saw Iris. It was amazing how she stood out. Her tricky ski costume was as exotic as they come, and yet, in spite of the glamour, there was an undefinable air of assurance. Anyone looking at her could have told that she was a champion skier. Which she was.

My first reaction was one of husbandly pride. My second — which should have been my first — was a quick stab of apprehension. Somehow, it was only then, when we were actually about to board the train, that I realized just how wantonly I was letting her plunge into danger. I had an absurd desire to catch up with her and force her to go back to the apartment out of harm's way. Then both my pride and my anxiety suffered a setback. Because she was not alone.

She was walking with a man. I saw his profile as he turned to look at her. He was very big, very blond, very handsome. A Scandinavian of some sort. He was carrying Iris's skis as well as his own, slung over his shoulder above his rucksack, as carelessly as toothpicks.

I felt a kind of fury and a kind of jealousy and a kind of hurt. After all, I'd been married to her only six months. Then, slowly, there was a grudging admiration, too. A "ski-instructor" before she had even boarded the train! My wife certainly was a fast worker.

Sulking, I stumped on up the platform to R. 18.

The berths hadn't been made down yet and the car was as festive as a fraternity common room. Strangers were already treating strangers like lifelong friends, tied together by the common bond of snow and slalom. Four college boys, exuberantly sharing a pint of rye, were giving a lusty performance of *The Last Roundup*; three show girls, who had obviously never seen a ski-slope, were trying to make three young men think Sun Valley was their Home from Home; two lean-faced men and a woman with strong hands and a Helen Hokinson figure were determinedly arguing the merits of various waxes on fast snow.

I dumped my skis with the pile of others in the little compartment just inside the entrance and weaved through the passengers to my seat. I sat down, and simultaneously was hit in the ear by an elbow. I looked up, to see a young man with tousled brown hair, intelligent eyes, and a slight boy's body. He was smiling apologetically. "Sorry," he said in a refreshingly un-Stephen-Dorn Middle West accent. "I've always had the most uncontrollable elbows."

He fixed his things, sat down opposite me, and pulled out a book from his ski jacket pocket. I saw the title. It was *What Maisie Knew*, by Henry James.

Suddenly I felt a queer kind of panic. So little to go on. A perfumed cigarette—and one didn't smoke in sleepers. A half-moon-shaped scar above the right wrist—and all wrists were hidden under the buttoned sleeves of ski jackets. And a voice.

That was all. A voice. One voice out of two hundred and fifty skiers.

Outside someone was shouting. A whistle blew. The car, with its enthusiastic, chattering passengers, seemed suddenly unreal, ominous. What if I grabbed Iris and got off now? What ... ?

There was a groaning lurch. A forward jerk. And, outside the window, the platform started slipping slowly backward. The Ski-Monarch was under way....

I SAT THERE, having absolutely no sort of plan. The Hokinson woman, still talking with a passionate knowledge of skiing which her figure belied, had produced a *Bundles for Britain* bag and was knitting like mad. Her voice trailed across to me: "It's all right on the Hurricane Trail, but it would be crazy to try it on the Ramp. The terrain ..."

The Ramp! It came to me then, a half-buried recollection released by that chance remark. In the frankfurter note Hilda had written: *Transfer 10 a.m. northern foot of Ramp.* Until then that had meant nothing to me. A bus transfer? A station ramp? But now it meant everything. The Hurricane Trail wound precipitously down a mountain called Laurel Mountain. But right up against it, virtually on the Canadian border, was another mountain, a bare, sheer, ugly mountain which, by its queer contour, managed to dominate the whole countryside. I remembered that mountain well. But until then I had entirely forgotten its name.

The Ramp—of course.

So that was to be the crucial spot. 10 A. M. Tomorrow morning? Tomorrow morning, at the northern foot of that ominous mountain, Stephen Dorn was going to make a transfer. A transfer! Surely my original hunch had been right. Some sort of smuggling across the border. But smuggling of what? I thought of Huysmans, one of New York's biggest diamond magnates.

Diamonds ... !

Across the aisle the young man with the tousled hair slammed his Henry James shut, grinned at me, and said, "Maisie always works like a charm. Two pages of what she knew and I need a drink."

He got up and strolled down the aisle toward the rear of the train, presumably in search of the bar car. I sat on alone, feeling a mounting excitement. Locate Dorn and Dickie, watch them like a hawk, and then, tomorrow morning at ten o'clock ...

I needed a drink. Then I would be all set for action.

I MOVED UNSTEADILY down the aisle and out onto the rocking platform, where the cold air came up and where the train became suddenly a rushing, clattering missile, roaring northward through the snow, instead of a bright, static coach.

Finally I reached a compartment car for the really swanky skiers. I squeezed down the narrow, deserted corridor, the train jolting me against the closed doors of the compartments. I had almost come to the end of it when I heard the door from the next car opening. From where I was I couldn't see around the corner to who was coming in. But I heard a voice, a husky, agitated woman's voice, saying, "I told you we shouldn't go to the bar."

I may not have recognized that voice the night before, when I answered Anstey's telephone. But now it was indelibly stamped on my memory.

Juliana!

I was right opposite the washroom. I ducked through the green curtain into the little empty room. I heard footsteps in the corridor coming closer and closer. Then Huysmans's voice, soft, unemotional: "Why worry? He doesn't know anything about us."

And then Juliana, urgently: "I know. But just seeing him there in the bar scares me."

The voices faded with the footsteps.

Just seeing him there in the bar! I felt a tingling of excitement. I started to push back the curtain and move out of the washroom. But I didn't. My hand dropped to my side. I stood quite still, the hairs at the back of my neck stirring. I hadn't noticed it before. I guess I had been entirely absorbed with Juliana and Huysmans. But now it trailed through the stale air toward me—a sweet, sickly perfume, a perfume which brought back with horrible vividness the small hours of the morning, the snowy basement of 135A East 69th Street, fear, and that soft, cultured, loathsome voice.

I turned. I stared at the row of wash-basins, the bare leather couch, the ash tray on its tall metal stand. Resting on the edge of the ash tray, sending a small, blue spiral of smoke up into the air, was a cigarette butt. I went to it. I picked it up, the perfume invading my nostrils. I read the small, gold letters around its base: *Fortuna.*

Just seeing him there in the bar scares me. A Fortuna cigarette butt.... This was too easy. Stephen Dorn had just been here in the washroom. Stephen Dorn had just gone to the bar.

I hurried out and onto the platform leading to the next car. I looked through the plate-glass window into the car beyond. It was the bar car itself, the last car on the train.

This was certainly too easy!

Out of the two hundred and fifty-odd skiers on the Ski-Monarch, a wild coincidence had narrowed Stephen Dorn down to one of the handful beyond me there in the bar.

I stood on the rocking platform, my hand on the door, feeling a kind of stage fright. Then I tugged open the door and stepped into the bar.

I saw my friend with the tousled hair and the Henry James standing at the bar. He saw me and waved. I saw another single man at the bar. A dark, Italianate young man who, for one unpleasant moment, I thought was Alessandro. He wasn't. I saw an indeterminate youth with pale eyes and a red-haired girl sipping what looked like Cuba Libres at one of the tables. And then, with a violent jolt, I saw Iris and her Scandinavian.

THEY WERE SITTING at the center table of the car. The Scandinavian had his broad, blond back to me. But I could see Iris's face. She saw me, too. But she paid me no attention. She was leaning over a liqueur brandy, gazing into the Scandinavian's eyes as if they were deep, unmined fiords.

Cynthia Rowley, indeed!

And then, while my indignation was simmering, I saw the only other occupants of the bar. They, too, were sitting at a table together. They were both drinking highballs. They were both men. Both youngish men. New Yorkish, actorish young men. One with very large, dark eyes, too much dark hair, and the sleeves of his ski jacket buttoned tightly around his wrists. The other, pink and boyish and frank-eyed with the sort of calculated unsophistication of someone who has learned that being pink and boyish and frank-eyed pays dividends.

Because I couldn't just stand there, I joined my Henry James friend at the bar. He put his book down and said, "Maisie's done it again. Two more pages and I'm set for another drink. What'll you have?"

"Scotch and soda," I said.

I glanced at the Italianate young man beyond us at the bar. He seemed bored and rather miserable and completely indifferent.

The drinks came. The young man with the tousled hair went on talking amiably, but I wasn't really paying attention. I was thinking: Eight people in the car. Six men—Henry James, the Italian, the man with the redhead, Iris's Scandinavian, and the two ornate young men in the corner.

Six men—one of them Stephen Dorn.

It was a queer, creepy sensation, knowing he was there in that little group—the man who had tried to kill me, the man who would try even more vigorously to kill me if he knew that I, the man with the curious nose and the Scotch and soda, was Peter Duluth.

How to narrow him down without arousing suspicion? That was the problem. I was working on it when, suddenly, disastrously, I heard a female voice behind me, caroling, ecstatic: "Is it? Can it be? Yes, yes it is. Peter, *darling* … !"

The bar seemed to sway around me. I didn't dare turn around.

"Peter, but how *divine!*"

There was one awful moment of suspense. Then I felt a hand clutch my sleeve. I turned, staring dizzily at a spectacular blonde. There was another blonde with her. They were both dazzling me with smiles.

I felt something sink through me like a plummet. Why did I have to be a Broadway producer and know every bit actress in town? Particularly actresses who had worked with me like this—what was her name?—Amanda Bell.

Amanda Bell was pulling the other blonde forward. Escape was utterly impossible. "Peter, this is Gloria West. Gloria, this is Peter Duluth." The name seemed to boom around the bar like an explosion. "*The* Peter Duluth, you know. Really the most divinely handsome important man on Broadway." Her laughter tinkled. "Do you know, Peter, for a moment I didn't recognize you? It's your nose. What have you done to your nose? Really, it's rather divine."

That "Peter Duluth" still seemed to roar around the car. I was acutely conscious of the fact that everyone was staring at us; the two young men glancing up under their lashes; the redhead and her boy-friend frankly curious; Iris's Scandinavian turning his head to give me a long, blond gaze. Even the Italian shifted out of his lethargy and shot me a swift olive glance.

Only Iris remained studiedly uninterested. And, as the ground crumbled under my feet, that was one slight straw to cling to. Amanda Bell hadn't known me since my marriage. At least, she wouldn't recognize Iris.

"Peter, darling, this is too heavenly. Tell me all about yourself. Are you producing this season? Are you ... ?"

I just couldn't cope with them. I could only think how devastatingly the tables had been turned, how somewhere around me in the car Stephen Dorn was watching me; Stephen Dorn, whom I had narrowed down to one of six men; Stephen Dorn, who now had very definitely narrowed me down to—one of one men.

From now on the dice were loaded against me. From now on I would be living, breathing, and sleeping—danger.

Mumbling something incoherent, I walked out on Amanda and Gloria. I left them flat. I hurried out of the bar car. And I didn't look at anyone as I went. Not even at "Cynthia Rowley." ...

WHEN I GOT back, shakily, to my sleeper, the gaiety was over. Skiers keep early hours. Almost all the berths had been made down, the cheerful, tavern atmosphere had already been transformed into the curtained bleakness of a sleeper at night. The train roared and rattled. It was all very dour.

I asked the porter to make down my berth. Now that I had become the quarry again after my brief fling as the hound, it seemed wisest to go to earth. While the porter was fussing around, I unearthed a toothbrush and went to the washroom. I wasn't going to risk exhibiting myself in the aisle.

There, in the washroom, I started thinking what Dorn's next move was liable to be. Would he try to kill me right away, here on the crowded ski-train? Surely not. A corpse in R. 18 would mean inevitable delay. And delay would be fatal to the rendezvous at 10 A. M. at the foot of the Ramp. No. It was far more likely that he would bide his time until we reached our destination.

That was a little comforting. With any luck I still had one more night to live!

When I got back to my place, my berth had been made. "Henry James" had returned from the bar. His berth was being made down, too. He grinned at me quizzically and said, in his Western twang, "You certainly walked out on those two blondes."

I grinned back weakly. I don't know why. Muttering "Good night," I pushed back the green curtains of my lower and squeezed into my bunk.

I had decided against undressing. There is something so defenseless about pajamas. Flapping the curtains shut behind me, I wriggled over on the narrow bed, so that I lay flat on my back. I didn't relish the prospect of the night ahead of me. I didn't relish it at all. Fool's venture! I couldn't have christened this expedition more aptly.

If only I had brought something to read. I thought then of my friend in the lower berth across the aisle with his *What Maisie Knew*. Solid, sober Henry James. Just the thing.

I pushed my curtains aside. The little light was on in his berth. I called softly, "Hi."

His voice replied immediately, "What?"

"I want to read. How about lending me *Maisie*?"

"Sure."

I saw his curtains tremble. Then his bare arm came out, stretching the book across the aisle. I leaned forward to take it. He was in pajamas. As he stretched toward me, the pajama sleeve crinkled up, revealing his bare arm.

I TOOK THE BOOK. But I was hardly conscious of what I was doing. For, in the dim light of the sleeper aisle, I was staring at "Henry James's" bare right arm. Just under the wrist, where before it had been concealed by the buttoned sleeve of his ski jacket, I saw a blue, thin scar shaped like a half-moon.

Somehow my voice said, "Thank you."

The arm which fascinated and repelled me slipped back through the curtains. I slipped back through my own.

Maisie was quivering in my hand like a feather in a high wind. So much for my brilliant deductions from cigarette butts and overheard conversations! So much for my fool's venture to the bar! All the time Stephen Dorn had been the man in the lower next to mine—the young man with the tousled hair, the intelligent eyes, and the friendly smile, the one person on the train whom I had been prepared to trust.

And I had trusted him because he spoke with a Middle Western accent. As a detective I was still a good play producer. Naturally, if you had a voice as distinctive as Dorn's you would disguise it when traveling incognito. A Middle Western accent is not difficult to assume.

I didn't sleep much that night. For hour after rattling hour, I lay there reading *What Maisie Knew* grimly. Every now and then I dozed off. But not for long. I was awake when the first finger of light crept through under the curtain which screened the window. I was awake an hour later when the Ski-Monarch slowed down, shuddered, and stopped. I glanced at my watch. 7:30 A. M. We had arrived.

For a few moments I lay there, collecting myself against the day. This was where the danger really began. In two and a half hours the "transfer" was to take place. Some time during those two and a half hours, Dorn and Dickie—where was Dickie?—would presumably make an attempt to remove the one person whom they thought of as George and Hilda's associate. Those two and a half hours craved very wary walking by Peter Duluth.

Most of my fears had gone with the night. I felt almost calm—for myself. But I didn't feel calm for Iris. Somehow I had to get in touch with her, let her know who Dorn was, and warn her to keep the hell out of it.

Around me I was conscious of the dull, morning voices of awakened sleepers. There were clatterings in the aisle. I pulled back my curtains. Across the way, Dorn's curtains were still drawn. Here was my chance.

I slipped out, shaking some of the night creases from my ski clothes. I picked up my rucksack, slid *Maisie* onto the floor outside Dorn's lower, and joined the earliest skiers who were searching for their own skis in the bristling ski-compartment....

There was a dramatic thrill to that first moment of Vermont. Virgin slopes of snow stretched around us indefinitely, dwarfing the little New England station and the straggling village into child's toys. And beyond, gleaming-white and pine-tree dark in swathes, were the mountains. I could make out the massive bulk of Laurel Mountain. And, yes, behind it, squat, ugly, pushing up like a great thumb—the Ramp.

Three busses were crouched in the snow behind the station to take us to the Mountain Inn at the very foot of the Hurricane Trail. Around me, skiers were crowding toward them, their breath making gray balloons in the crisp morning air. I followed, scanning unfamiliar faces urgently for Iris. I reached the busses. There was no sign of her.... And then she came around the side of the station, beautiful, self-possessed—and accompanied by her Scandinavian.

I started toward her. Scandinavian boyfriend or no, I had to warn her about Dorn. I had almost reached her, almost opened my mouth to speak, when she saw me. And, in a flash her face went cold and unyielding as stone. For one second her eyes pierced straight through me. Then swiftly she turned to the Scandinavian. She smiled at him. In a loud, distinct voice she said, "A perfect skiing day, Dickie. Oh, Dickie, I'm so excited!"

Dickie! With a certain wildness, just in the nick of time, I swerved away. Iris linked her hand through Dickie's large arm and they got on one of the busses.

I STOOD THERE in the snow with my skis, my nerves jangling like cowbells. So this was Iris's train pickup. Somehow she had identified Dickie from the start, and that was the reason for her high-power vamping act. It hadn't just been to make me mad! The fool, the crazy little fool—didn't she realize the danger? Didn't she ... ?

At that moment I felt a hand on my shoulder. I looked around, and there was Stephen Dorn. He looked at me with those slanted, intelligent eyes beneath the tousled hair. "Well, how did you enjoy *What Maisie Knew?*"

"She knew too much," I said.

He smiled that frank, boyish smile which now, to me, was infinitely sinister. "So did Hilda," he said.

So he was coming straight out with it now! There was to be no more pretense. We stared at each other squarely, there in the snow—two antagonists measuring each other's strength.

I'm afraid he won. I was still too jittery about Iris. He slipped his arm almost affectionately over my shoulder, the arm with the half-moon scar under the ski-jacket. "I'm going to enjoy this ski-trip. Come on. Let's get on a bus."

On the bus he sat next to me, bottling me up against the window. And for all of the fifteen miles of journey through the snowy roads to the Mountain Inn he talked to me banteringly, almost caressingly, glancing at me out of the corners of his eyes. Stephen Dorn certainly knew his war-of-nerves technique.

Not that my nerves needed any extra work. Iris had completely undermined me. I could take care of myself, even with a toy revolver. But the idea of Iris playing with fire made me almost sick with apprehension. How to get her out of it? I couldn't even speak to her now without tripling the danger for her. As the bus and Dorn rattled on, I thought wildly of calling the police, whatever the cost to myself. But I saw at once how hopeless it would be. I had nothing against Dorn. Absolutely nothing.

I thought of Juliana and Huysmans then. And I clung to the thought of them like a drowning man to a floating beer keg. Juliana and Huysmans knew what this fantastic thing was all about. Judging from the $10,000 check, they were as desperately eager as I to sabotage Dorn. Then cooperate with them. Maybe there was something there. At least, I could try.

They weren't on our bus. But when we reached the Mountain Inn—a huge, rambling clapboard affair nestling in the shadow of Laurel Mountain—I managed to shake Dorn off in the throng of skiers. I pushed my way into the crowded lounge, with its heavy beams and bright, welcoming fires. Breakfast was being served, and most of the skiers were headed for the dining-room. Probably Juliana and Huysmans.... Then I saw them. They were hurrying up the stairs with a bellboy carrying their things.

I glanced at my watch. Almost nine o'clock. Only an hour to go. Not caring whether Dorn saw me or not, I dashed up the stairs. I saw the bellboy coming out of a room at the end of the corridor. I ran to it. The door was still open. Without even knocking, I pushed through it, skis, rucksack, and all.

Juliana and Huysmans both swung round. Juliana's exotic face went blank, and then white with anxiety. "Peter—you here!"

Huysmans was staring at me, as impassive as ever. "I advised you to keep out of this, Mr. Duluth."

"If I could keep out of it do you suppose I'd be here?" I hadn't much of a plan. Rather wildly I said, "You've got to let me in with you. I'm in danger. My wife's in danger. You've got to tell me exactly what's going to happen at ten o'clock at the foot of the Ramp."

Juliana looked Dutch and voluptuous and hostile. Huysmans said coldly, "It is nothing that concerns you."

"It concerns me plenty." I saw a telephone by the window. I went to it, theatrically. "If you don't tell me I'll call the police and report everything I know."

Huysmans knew I was bluffing. He didn't bat an eyelid. "If you call the police, Mr. Duluth, I shall let them know that you are wanted in New York for the murder of George Anstey."

THAT HAD ME STOPPED. Outside the window the great bulk of Laurel Mountain reared up, with the sheer white strip of the Hurricane Trail sweeping dizzily down its side, to end in a wide slope just back of the hotel porch. Farther off, looming squatly behind the flank of Laurel Mountain, I made out the Ramp.

That made me conscious of the time element—desperately. I took a brodie. "It's no use holding out on me, anyway. Because I know. It's diamonds, isn't it? Dorn's smuggling diamonds in from Canada. And you're trying to stop him." I went on jerkily: "At the moment Dorn thinks I'm his enemy, that I'm the person who bought off Hilda and George. That's why there's danger to me. What if I told him you were the people really to watch out for? What about that?"

That approach only came to me on the spur of the moment, but it worked like a charm. Juliana gave a stifled gasp.

Huysmans looked, for him, almost emotional. "So it is your turn now, Mr. Duluth, to be aiming the revolver. If you were to make Dorn suspicious of us, it would be so disastrous that—" He shrugged wearily. "Exactly what is it you want?"

"Safety for my wife and myself. And the whole dope on the transfer at the foot of the Ramp."

"I have no way of ensuring your safety." Huysmans moistened his lips. "And there is no need to tell you about the transfer, since you seem to know already."

"Then it is diamond smuggling." I felt suddenly exasperated. "Here I have been framed for murder, shot at, hounded into an impossible situation—just because a bunch of crooks are squabbling over hot diamonds."

"You also managed to make ten thousand dollars out of your misfortunes," said Huysmans acidly. I didn't tell him Iris had torn up the check. "And I would prefer not to have you call us crooks. Miss Guilder and I are here with no thought of personal gain. We are only doing what little we can to help our native country."

I stared. "You—you mean you're foreign agents or … ?"

"No, Peter. Nothing so dramatic. Just ordinary people trying to keep bad things from getting worse." Juliana came to me, laying her hand on my arm urgently. She looked beautiful then—and nice, too. I almost understood why I used to like her. "You know, Derek and I were both born in Holland. You know the ghastly thing that has happened to it, swallowed up by an enemy army, crippled ..."

"Juliana," cut in Huysmans sharply.

"Oh, let me tell him. If he knows the truth he'll have to see how important it is." Juliana's eyes were pleading. "Yes, Peter, diamonds are coming across the border at ten. Thousands and thousands of dollars' worth of them. But they're not just diamonds. They're the lawful property of the Dutch government, diamonds appropriated by the invaders. Derek still has an underground way of contacting Holland. A few weeks ago he heard about it—heard that the diamonds were being smuggled over to Canada by enemy agents posing as Dutch refugees. They're going to be sold here in the States. Smuggled across and sold for American dollars. Dollars that are infinitely important for the enemy."

I'D THOUGHT OF it as a purely personal thing of crook against crook. This, with its overtones of general calamity, was something far more terrifying.

"And Dorn," I stammered, "is the man who's going to take over the selling of them in this country?"

"Yes." Juliana's voice was fierce. "Stephen Dorn isn't really a professional criminal. He's much, much more dangerous. Very intelligent, utterly cynical, ready to work for anyone, provided there's enough in it for him. Anstey and Hilda Purvis were small-time crooks working for him, posing as private investigators. Their job was to contact potential purchasers, and they were stupid enough to go to Derek. That's how he got onto Dorn. And, just by paying them more, we won them over to our side. They got murdered for it yesterday. But we got the information, and Dorn doesn't suspect we even know."

Huysmans came forward, still very stiff. "Perhaps you see now what you would be doing if you warned Dorn,

Mr. Duluth. You would not only be dealing Holland yet another crushing blow, you would also be seriously injuring your own country by letting thousands upon thousands of dollars of American currency fall into the hands of a foreign and hostile power." He looked at me earnestly. "As an American, apart from anything else, I can surely rely on you not to warn Dorn."

That made my own personal problems, however perilous, seem rather small. "Of course you can rely on me. But, if it's as big as this, you should get in the police and ..."

"We are taking all the necessary steps, Mr. Duluth." Huysman's voice was very cold. "Perhaps I can ask one more favor. Since Dorn is suspicious of you, it might be fatal if you were seen talking to us. I must ask you to avoid us completely in these crucial moments." He paused. "As for your personal safety, you have blundered into something far more important than you. And you must blunder out again. I can advise only one thing: Take a room and lock yourself in—until this is all over."

"But ..." I began.

"There is really nothing more to say."

I couldn't have been dismissed more peremptorily by Queen Wilhelmina herself.

I slipped out of the room and moved down the dark, deserted corridor to the head of the stairs. In the vestibule below I could hear the festive chatter of skiers departing for the Hurricane Trail. I knew the secret now. Grim and crucial as it was, at least it made sense. I was no longer drifting in a world of darkness and mystery. But things were no better. Somehow Juliana and Huysmans had taken "all necessary steps" to get Dorn. Presumably without the aid of the police. If they succeeded, that would be dandy for Holland, dandy for everyone—except me. My fingerprints in Anstey's apartment would still involve me hopelessly with the law, and Dorn was still as great a menace as ever.

And then there was Iris—Iris, in her casual, girlish way, flirting with an international crook and mortal danger.

I LOOKED AT my watch. Nine-fifteen. Only three quarters of an hour to go. I felt a sort of engulfing panic. While I had been fussing with Huysmans and Juliana, Dorn and Dickie had probably already started on their way to the Ramp. And Iris! My heart was thumping. What of her? She was just crazy enough to have followed them.

Huysmans or no Huysmans, there could be no locked room for me until Iris was safe. Recklessly, not caring whether each and every step on the Mountain Inn staircase was mined, I started down to the vestibule. As I went, I scanned the crowd of skiers below for Iris. I didn't see her. But I saw something infinitely less nice.

Lounging at the bottom of the stairs, with their skis over their shoulders, watching my descent calmly, were Stephen Dorn—and Dickie.

I couldn't have avoided them, however much I wanted to. Which was plenty. Dorn came up the stairs to me. He smiled straight into my face with that frank, friendly smile—that Stalin smile which said, "I've got everything figured out, and wouldn't you like to know what it is?"

"I thought we'd lost you for good, Mr. Duluth," he said silkily. The Middle Western accent had been packed away with Henry James now. This was the real, smooth, cultured, unpleasant Voice. Dickie came up behind him. Dorn turned to him. "And this—in case you haven't identified him already—is Dickie Swanson."

I suppose it was instructive to know that Dickie's name was Swanson. He showed a lot of white Scandinavian teeth and gripped my hand in a Judas grip. I was thinking: At least, Iris isn't with them. That's something. At least, they can't do me any damage in this crowded vestibule. That was something, too.

Dorn was still smiling. "Well, Duluth, since you've come all this way to be with us, we weren't going to start without you. Come along, and we'll all take the Hurricane Trail together."

What was I supposed to make of that? I stared stupidly.

"Don't be worried," said Dorn. "I assure you we neither of us have guns. See for yourself." He propped his skis against the banister and raised his hands mockingly over his head. Dickie did the same thing. Although it was all quite mad, I—in Alessandro's parlance—"frisked" them both. Dorn was speaking the truth. Neither of them carried a revolver.

I WAS STRUGGLING to find some sense somewhere when suddenly everything went out of my mind. Because I saw Iris. She was pushing through the skiers, her skis over her shoulder, coming straight toward us. I tried to shoot her a warning glance. She paid no attention. She came up the stairs, slipped her arm through Dickie's, smiled at him dazzlingly, and said, "Here you are, Dickie! Come on; let's get out on the trail."

Dickie looked awkward. I felt as if a fox was at my entrails.

"Well," Dickie began, "you see, I kind of promised these …"

"Lovely!" Iris was radiantly calm. "Let's all go together. And, by the way, introduce me."

Flushing a deep red, Dickie mumbled some name for Dorn. And Dorn, as calm as Iris, nodded to me and said, "This is Mr. Duluth."

"Not *the* Mr. Duluth!" Iris quoted Amanda Bell, round-eyed. "The most divinely handsome important man on Broadway!"

I had to take it. I wanted to scream at her. The little fool. What did she think this was? A suicide pact? But I couldn't do anything. That was the agony of it. It was all up to Dickie and Dorn. Which meant, of course, Dorn.

He took it in his stride—horribly in his stride, as though Iris's demented injection of herself suited his plan to perfection.

"Fine, Miss Rowley," he said. "Come on. Let's all get going."

So there I was, hog-tied. I couldn't cry off and let Iris go on alone. I had no choice but to take the plunge. My own idea had been to keep my wife out of danger. And this was what she had done to me!

We all put on our skis. We started for the tow—just as if we were ordinary skiers instead of two murderers, their would-be victim, and their would-be victim's lunatic wife in disguise. All the time, that one thought was hammering in my head: What is their plan? How does Iris affect it? What is their plan?

We passed the broad practice slope at the end of the train, which was already crowded with the less ambitious skiers, and went on to the tow. It started some hundred yards from the foot of the trail itself and went through a cutting in the trees straight up the side of the mountain. To me there is always something rather macabre about a ski-tow with its animated clothesline moving slowly, remorselessly upward with a kind of skeleton El. Now, as we waited our turn, gripped straps, and started being pulled up, I had an exaggerated dentist's waiting-room sensation.

Each foot up, each minute that slid by, was taking us nearer—what?

Bobbing ahead of us on the towline, were the Hokinson woman and her two boyfriends. Turning back, looking dizzily down toward the hotel, I saw—of all people—the blond Amanda Bell and the blonder Gloria West hanging on their straps like seasoned experts. And I had assumed that their only skiing had been done on magazine covers.

Iris was ahead, then Dickie, then Dorn, and then me. The other three were chattering calmly about Telemark versus Christie. I couldn't bear it. The rest of that trip up the mountain was a kind of blur—a nightmare blur.

WE REACHED THE top of Laurel Mountain and joined the little group of skiers standing there, smoking cigarettes, chatting before they took the plunge down the trail. Through the lightly falling snow there was a breath-taking eagle's view of the valley, and, beyond it, the sister range of mountains, wooded and bare in strips, over across the border in Canada. About fifty yards below us the bare slope became wooded and the mouth of the Hurricane Trail yawned darkly through the trees. And to our left, lower than us, the peak of the Ramp was visible—bare, treeless, and infinitely lonely.

One after another, the skiers started dropping away down the bare, snowy slope, headed toward the mouth of the Hurricane. I saw the Hokinson woman go off with her two men, swinging her hips in as pretty a set of Christies as I hope to see. But none of it seemed real. It was all part of the horror fantasy of Dorn, Dickie, Iris—clustered around me, smoking, laughing.

I glanced at my watch. Dorn saw me glancing. Twenty of ten!

And then Dorn said, "Well, let's at it. Dickie and Miss Rowley, you start the ball rolling. See if you can't race him, Miss Rowley."

Iris looked at me then. I looked at her. I could read nothing in her expression. "Okay," she said. "Fifty cents on it, Dickie." And she glided away down the slope.

Dickie glanced at Dorn, hesitated a moment, and then started off with a flick of his black ski poles.

I watched them, thinking of every possible disaster. Iris was in beautiful form, skimming like a swallow. Dickie was good, too. But not so good.

Dorn and I were there. We weren't alone. There was still a little huddle of skiers around us. He smiled at me. "There's more than fifty cents on our race, isn't there, Mr. Duluth? Much more." He gave a derisive little bow. And he was off.

I stood there, staring stupidly. Nothing meant anything any more. Iris and Dickie had slid into the mouth of the trail, out of sight. Dorn was skiing like a wizard. Elegant as they come.

What to do? Quarter of ten. What to do?

Then, behind me, I heard familiar, ecstatic voices: "Peter, darling! ... Yoohoo, Mr. Duluth ... !"

Amanda and Gloria. That decided me. I slipped my ski poles off my wrists into my palms, pushed myself forward, and followed down the slope after Dorn.

I was a bit unsteady at first. Nerves, mostly, and lack of practice. But soon the feel of the skis against the snow surface brought me confidence. The mouth of the Trail loomed closer. I stemmed into it. It was fairly narrow and dazzlingly white between the dark walls of pines. But this first stretch was straight for a couple of hundred feet. I was just in time to catch a glimpse of Iris's ski suit before she disappeared around the far bend. I saw Dickie lagging behind her. And, not so far in front of me, Dorn.

I followed, the crisp air whistling past my ears, my eyes glued on the two skiers ahead. And then, just before he reached the bend around which Iris had vanished, Dickie swerved left and zoomed down a sidetrack out of sight. A couple of seconds later Dorn reached the same spot. He too, stemmed sharp left—down the same little trail.

I SAW THEIR game then. At least, some of it. From the start they had planned to take the Hurricane tow and tack off cross-country to the Ramp. And Iris, who had injected herself against their wills, had been neatly shaken off. By lagging behind, Dickie had eluded her. Now she was going on down the Hurricane Trail, racing like mad to win her fifty cents. She was safe!

That gave me a wild sense of exhilaration. The little sidetrack grew closer and closer. Dorn and Dickie had deliberately taken me along with them. They had left me to ski last. They had made no attempt to hide their turnoff from me. That meant, almost certainly, that they wanted me to follow them—into some trap.

But I didn't care then. Iris was safe. They didn't have revolvers. They were only two against one. And if, by some miracle, I could outsmart them at the eleventh hour, the hopeless tangle of my relationship with the world, the police, and the devil might be straightened out peaceably—forever.

Of course, there was danger. Of course, Dorn was smart. Of course a thousand things ... But my blood was up then. Dorn, Dickie, Juliana, Huysmans ... pooh!

Recklessly I Christied into the turnoff.

It wasn't a real trail, just a narrow path through the trees. Dickie and Dorn were not in sight, but their tracks stretched clearly ahead of me. My heart jumping, I started to follow them, weaving to and fro, going as fast as I could. Soon I had left the Hurricane Trail, with its life, its other skiers, its safety, far behind.

Suddenly the woods stopped and I was on a bare, snowy slope with a vast panorama of the Canadian mountains, dominated by the great bulk of the Ramp to my left. The ski-tracks headed straight down the slope. I could see them plainly plunging down and, at the foot, sheering left around a thick patch of hemlocks, out of sight. A slight rise at the end of the slope kept me from seeing what lay beyond. But I didn't pay much attention, anyway. All I cared about was the tracks, veering left toward the Ramp.

I pushed off and started schussing down the slope. I picked up immense speed. It was thrilling just as a physical sensation. Careering down, I reached the spot where the tracks swerved left around the hemlocks. I went into a Christie, zooming around the hemlocks, losing scarcely any pace.

And then it happened. In one terrifying split second I saw the dead limb thrown across the track ahead of me; in that same split second I saw that the ground to my right dropped sheer away in a precipice.

If I had stopped to think, to plan, I would have swerved or crashed and been lost. But I didn't. Obeying some blind instinct, my arms went out, my poles dug into the snow barely six inches from the limb, and, throwing myself up in a gelaendesprung, I cleared the hazard and landed on the other side of it. I tried to go into a Telemark stop, but I failed and collapsed sideways into the hemlocks.

It was only then, as I lay panting and tangled in the hemlocks with the danger past, that I had time to be terrified. There was reason enough. The track was scarcely five feet wide and completely blocked by the limb. Pushing myself up, I peered over the edge of the precipice. There was a straight drop, a drop which no human body could have taken and remained intact.

So this had been Dorn's little plan for my demise! This was why he had been able so ostentatiously to dispense with guns! Very clever and very simple for anyone who knew the terrain as they must know it. I had been deliberately lured into following. And then, ten seconds to drag the dead limb out of the hemlock outcrop and throw it across the track were all Dorn had needed to stage a hazard with a hundred-to-one chance of hurling me to my doom. And a most ingenious doom, too. My body, if it had crashed over, would have been lost to sight in the snowdrifts below probably for weeks. And, even if it were found, the death would almost certainly have been written off as just another skiing accident.

That the miracle had happened and I had escaped without a bruise was just so much bad luck—or good luck, depending on how you looked at it.

The ski tracks stretching unbrokenly onward along the edge of the precipice showed me—much to my relief—that they hadn't waited to see their prey fall into the trap. This omission must have been due either to Dorn's overweening confidence or, which was more likely, to the fact that they hadn't been able to afford the time. After all, it was almost ten o'clock.

As I stood there, still breathing jerkily, I stared down the trail ahead. There was one little rise, and then beyond it, thrusting out to the right, stretching down into a desolate valley, the Ramp itself.

The northern foot of the Ramp! There it was right in front of me. Graciously, by failing to kill me, Dorn had given me a ringside seat. Without moving an inch from the shadow of the hemlocks, I would be able to witness the transfer itself.

And then, as I watched, two small, black figures came into my range of vision from behind the little slope ahead, two figures skimming down the long slope of the Ramp toward the valley ... Dorn and Dickie. ... And, perfectly timed, as if obeying some theater cue, I saw a third figure, far up the slope on the other side of the valley, a solitary skier, tiny, dwarfed into nothingness by the immensity of the surrounding waste.

THIS, THEN, WAS the transfer! Vaguely I had expected melodrama — Juliana, Huysmans, hoards of customs men on skis swarming in all directions.

And there was just this. Two figures skiing down one slope. One figure skiing down another. I saw then how classically simple and inspired Dorn's plan had been. Two lone skiers casually meeting a third — "by chance." Two skiers going back to their harmless ski-party. Two skiers enjoying a pleasant week end at the Mountain Inn. Two skiers returning inconspicuously to New York on a holiday ski-train.

If it hadn't been for the watchful patriotism of Juliana and Huysmans, the venality of George and Hilda, and my own fool's blundering, who would have guessed that in those mild, everyday incidents a vast, illicit fortune had changed hands and countries?

Dickie and Dorn were almost at the foot of the Ramp. Suddenly they disappeared from sight behind a little rise I hadn't noticed before. The lone skier had almost reached them. He, too, disappeared.

Almost before I realized it, I saw the lone skier again plodding his way back up the slope he had come down. And then, a few seconds later, there were Dorn and Dickie starting back up the Ramp.

The transfer had been as easy as that!

The "accident" and the transfer had followed each other in such swift, distracting succession that there had been next to no time to think about my immediate future. Now, suddenly, its urgency was forced upon me. What to do?

Almost certainly Dorn and Dickie would return this way. They would want to get back to the Hurricane Trail and, certainly, they would have to inspect their trap.

IT WAS THEN that the idea sprang fully fledged into my mind. It was a crazy, wild idea, but there was a chance of its coming off.

Dorn and Dickie were coming past this actual spot with the diamonds on them. And they expected me to be dead. Okay. I would be dead. It was very simple. My tracks where I had jumped the limb were pretty scuffed up, anyway. I scuffed them some more, taking them right to the edge of the precipice. Then, a final artistic touch, I tossed my ski cap down in the melee, as if it had flown from my head as I went careering to my doom. When I was through, the tableau was pretty convincing.

Now all I had to do was to ambush myself in the hemlocks. They had no revolvers. I had a toy revolver. People had held up banks before now with toy revolvers. Why shouldn't I be able to hold up Dorn and Dickie? Not only hold them up but hustle them back to the hotel at pistol point and hand them over to the police. With them safely behind bars as smugglers and with a full report on the murders from me, I might yet come out of this affair unscathed.

Juliana and Huysmans, in spite of their assertions, weren't doing anything visibly constructive. And they had given me the sneer direct when I'd offered to help them, while Dorn had constantly and insultingly underestimated my ingenuity.

Well, I'd show them all. Iris's words of last night rang triumphantly in my memory: *Theatrical producer rounds up gang single-handed!*

I could still see Dorn and Dickie plodding up the side of the Ramp. It would be a good ten minutes before they reached me. I took off my skis. That way I was more mobile.

I hid them in the hemlocks and then slipped in among the soft branches, myself. I took out my prop revolver. It looked lethal enough to me. I felt excited and gay. This was where Peter Duluth crashed through.

The next ten minutes, while I lurked with my gun in the hemlocks, were a sort of pins-and-needles infinity. And then Dorn and Dickie came gliding up so noiselessly that I barely heard them before they slipped into my vision. Then I only saw them in patches, Dorn's profile and shoulders, Dickie's broad back and his brown bamboo ski poles. They had stopped by the limb.

Dickie said, "Look; the tracks going over the side and his cap!" He sounded rather awed. "Gosh! It worked. He was as dumb as you said he was, Steve."

Dorn, calmly, said, "Shove the limb over the edge, Dickie. We don't want anyone to see it. Might give them ideas."

The two of them slipped their poles onto their wrists, stooped, and sent the limb toppling over the precipice. That seemed to be my moment.

I stepped out of the hemlocks. I aimed the prop revolver. I said histrionically, "Not quite as dumb as you thought. How about handing over those diamonds and taking a little trip back to the hotel?"

They both stared, Dickie's Scandinavian face going blank with apprehension, Dorn's registering nothing except a rather nasty amusement. His slanted, intelligent eyes dropped from my face to the revolver. He said, "Neither am I quite as dumb as you think, Duluth. I know a prop revolver when I see one. Now, this, for example—" There was a hideous pause. Then he felt in his pocket and produced a gun. "This little number which my friend across the border just gave me is much more the real thing."

He aimed it at me, smiling. The toy revolver dropped limply from my hand.

"Now," he said, "we will have the unusual privilege of eliminating you twice."

Dickie was grinning. They both were. Exasperation and shattered pride almost engulfed the realization of danger. But not quite. I had enough sense to appreciate the fact that, once and for all, the fool's venture was going to be over.

"Since our first idea was a good one," Dorn was saying, "I think we might repeat it. Put on your skis. And then you can give us a little exhibition of skier falling accidentally over precipice."

I thought wildly of turning and running. But that was hopeless. Even if they didn't shoot me, they were on skis and I was on foot. Apart from the little clump of hemlock there were no sheltering trees near by. They would inevitably catch up with me before I could get back to the Hurricane. Dazedly, in a sort of stupor, I pulled my skis out of the hemlocks and put them on.

THE REVOLVER WAS still pointing. "Now, Mr. Duluth, go around the hemlocks onto the slope. Go a little way up to give the necessary momentum, and then—over the top."

I obeyed. I had to. I started herring-boning up the slope, wondering if anyone else had ever had their life come to so humiliating an end. Dickie and Dorn had come around the hemlocks too, revolver and all.

"That's far enough, Mr. Duluth."

The moment had come. I started to turn. And then, miraculously, like the sound of angel voices, I heard little screams and titters. At first I couldn't believe them. Then definitely they came again. Little girlish laughs and cries: "There they are! ... Peter, darling. ... Yoohoo ... !"

I couldn't believe it. I blinked. I looked up the slope ahead of me. Deep organ music seemed to flood through me in ecstatic diapason. There, schussing, stemming, weaving down the slope toward us were three beautiful, glamorous females. One of them was blond, one of them was blonder, and one of them was dark. And she was the most beautiful. Oh, heavens, she was the most beautiful!

Amanda, Gloria—and Iris.

I glanced derisively over my shoulder. I saw Dorn's face white with fury. I saw him hesitate and then—of all things—toss the revolver over the precipice. And then, in a wild group, the girls were upon us. Christieing into stops, chattering, clustering around us. The Marines to the rescue!

"Peter, how *divine!*" caroled Amanda.

"Mr. Duluth, how *too* divine!" caroled Gloria.

And Iris—Iris skiied down to the distracted Dickie. She slipped her arm through his arm with a pouting grimace. "Dickie, you should be ashamed, and you owe me fifty cents. I got all the way down the Trail before I knew you'd quit. And I'd never have found you if the girls"—she waved at Amanda and Gloria—"hadn't seen Mr. Duluth take the turnoff. We all came up on the tow to find you."

It still didn't seem real. "Yes," said Amanda. "All you men getting together! Come on; let's have some fun." She nestled against me. "And, Peter, Gloria and I can't wait to hear about the play."

I stared stupidly.

"Yes," put in Iris. "I was just telling Amanda and Gloria how you'd said you might have parts for them in your new play, Mr. Duluth. That's why we were all so keen to come and look for you."

I cottoned then. Dear Iris, divine, inspired Iris! What a magnificent way to save your husband. With a barricade of blondes. No one, not even Dorn, could eliminate me, one brunette, and two blondes.

Iris had done the greatest triple table-turning in history.

DORN AND DICKIE still seemed entirely without a plan. Iris was pulling Dickie forward. "No excuses this time. We'll all make the trail together again. Amanda, you take Mr. Duluth; Gloria, you take the other gentleman. "She laughed gaily. "And see none of them get away this time, girls. No more men's talk for them."

It worked. It was as simple as that. Each of us guarded by a beautiful and determined wardress, we started up the slope, we got to the top, we weaved down the little track through the trees. And, almost before my pulses had stopped fluttering from my narrow escape, we all of us debouched onto the Hurricane Trail, with its infinitely desirable skiers, skiing past us, epitomizing the great, big world of safety again.

"Come on, boys and girls." Gloria was dragging Dorn forward. With a coy little giggle she pushed him, and he started off down the slope. She went after him, schussing to keep up, like an expert.

"Dickie, it's you and me. And another fifty cents on this." Iris was smiling ineluctably at Dickie. He started off, too, unhappily. She followed.

"Come on, Amanda, *darling*." Amanda and I started off in pursuit, her blond hair gleaming like a canary's wing. I'd never loved anyone more in my life. Scarcely anyone. Only Iris.

Probably no one has ever gone down the treacherous Hurricane Trail with more abandon. In almost no time it seemed we had schussed, zoomed, hurtled down, and broken out onto the practice slope, which stretched, bright with skiers, down to the hotel itself.

I saw Dorn and Gloria ahead, going like mad. I saw Iris and Dickie, too. Dickie was a little ahead. Iris was speeding after him. Then suddenly, another skier loomed in front of her. She swerved, and crashed straight into Dickie. The two of them fell, sprawling in a pile of flying ski poles. But Iris was up like lightning, grabbing poles and off down the slope in a regular whirlwind. She seemed to be taking her fifty-cent race seriously.

So did Dickie. He was haring after her. Amanda and I joined in the chase.

Our velocity was so great that we skied straight over the flatlands, right up to the hotel porch. Amanda and I were only a minute or so after the others. I saw Dorn and Gloria reach the porch. I saw Iris, with Dickie hot in pursuit, reach it too, and then veer off around it, out of sight.

THEN, JUST AS Amanda and I were fifty feet from the hotel, everything seemed to go mad. The porch doors were thrown open. I saw two familiar figures: Juliana and Huysmans. And behind them, in an indefinite hoard, crowded men in official uniforms.

Customs officers!

Juliana pointed dramatically at Dorn and Dickie. They made a feeble attempt to ski off. But the customs men bristled with guns.

"Those are the men!" exclaimed Juliana. "Those are they. Arrest them."

And they were arrested. It was as simple a business as you'd ever seen. Before Amanda and I reached the porch, both Dorn and Dickie were surrounded by customs men.

"Search them!" ordered Huysmans crisply. "Skis and all. Take them inside."

Dorn and Dickie were taking off their skis under official aegis. Customs men were leading them, skis over their shoulders, into the porch. They disappeared.

It all couldn't have taken more than a couple of minutes.

So this was what Huysmans had meant by "necessary steps." It *had* involved the authorities. They had known Dorn and Dickie would come back to the hotel. They knew Dorn was suspicious of no one but me. And, all the time I had been risking my neck all over the map, they had been sitting quietly at home with a swarm of customs men!

Amanda was staring in horrified, blond amazement. "My!" she said.

That was as good a reaction as any.

I got rid of her, took off my skis, and hurried through the porch into the big vestibule lounge. Juliana and Huysmans were there. I was just in time to see the customs men shepherding Dorn and Dickie into an inner room. No one else was around except a hovering manager and a few waiters. All the skiers were out on the trail.

Juliana saw me, and looked anxious. "Peter, you were out there, too!"

"I certainly was."

Huysmans came to me. He said urgently, "You mean you actually saw the transfer?"

"From a distance."

"Thank heaven. Then the customs men will get them, all right." He hesitated. "There's a private drawing-room off the corner there. Come with us, Mr. Duluth. I want to hear everything."

We went into the private room. While they listened intently, I told my lurid saga.

Huysmans wasn't at all sympathetic. "Really, Mr. Duluth, how ridiculous! We had our plans set ever since we left New York. I told you that. The customs men had been contacted. We felt certain that Dorn's scheme was to come back to the hotel with the diamonds. We came up to be able to identify them, and the arrest was prepared to catch them red-handed. The other man across the border is being arrested, too." He was keyed up. "You might well have thrown everything out of gear."

That was all the credit I got for risking my life in every possible position. Sourly I said, "You didn't confide in me. How was I to know? I didn't even think you were going to bring the authorities in at all."

Juliana looked a little sorry for me. She said brightly, "Well it's all turned out for the best, anyway. And you were half right about the police. We didn't want to call them, in the first place. Our country needs funds quickly, very quickly. Now there'll be all sorts of delays, red tape, proving the real ownership of the diamonds, customs complications, the trial. It will slow things down. But we had no choice. This seemed the only safe way."

Huysmans was looking jerkily at his watch. "The captain of the customs men will report to me as soon as the diamonds are found."

We slumped into half-hostile, jittery silence. I was just beginning to realize the exquisite fact that it was all over. A nice little arrest, lovely diamonds for Holland, and peace for Peter Duluth. At least, would there be peace? I thought nervously of the murders. Would Juliana and Huysmans be able to pin them on Dorn's gang, too?

That thought stayed like a gnat in my brain during that indefinite period while we waited for the customs captain. At last one of his men came. He looked rather flustered. "Captain James says will you come out into the vestibule."

We went out. Captain James was there with five other uniformed men and Dorn and Dickie. James looked as flustered as his minion. Dorn and Dickie looked very calm.

James said, "Mr. Huysmans, this is kind of awkward. We arrested these men on your tip-off because you said they had a lot of diamonds in their possession which they'd just smuggled over the border. We've searched 'em, clothes, skis, poles, everything. And we know how to search. We can find no diamonds on them at all."

Huysmans went white. Juliana went whiter. I felt almost the whitest of all.

James glanced at Dorn and Dickie. "Under the law, I have no authority to hold these men at all. They're carrying no guns. Nothing."

THERE WAS A very excruciating pause. I visualized Dorn being free, visualized the whole mad business starting up all over again. And I couldn't understand it. They *must* have got the diamonds from the lone skier. I had actually seen them meet. And they couldn't have hidden them on the way home. They hadn't had the chance, nor had they had any idea that the customs men would be waiting for them at the hotel.

Huysmans, utterly shaken, stammered, "Perhaps—perhaps they managed to conceal them somewhere along the trail. Yes, couldn't you hold them a little longer? Hold them until your men have searced the trail? They're dangerous criminals, I tell you. And the issue at stake is vital—vital."

James looked doubtful. "Well, maybe we could hold them a while and let the boys ..."

Just then the manager twittered up and said, "Phone call for you, Captain James."

James went away, and came back shortly. He looked rather stunned. He said to Huysmans, "You said these men are Stephen Dorn and Dickie Swanson?"

Huysmans nodded blankly.

James scratched his head. "If this ain't the craziest thing! That was the station calling. Phone message just came in from New York to arrest two guys called Dorn and Swanson. Some Italian, Alessandro something, was picked up in Washington and he squawked on them. Double murder."

Dorn stiffened. I gulped. I didn't believe it. Things just didn't come that pat.

"One of them, Dorn, has a scar on his right wrist, it said."

I gulped again. The captain went to Dorn and pulled back his ski-jacket sleeve. "Well, I guess this fixes it." He grinned at the startled Huysmans. "Sorry about that phony diamond charge, but it turned out dandy. Thanks for getting our men for us."

While we all preserved a staggered silence, there was a glint of handcuffs. Captain James and his followers hustled Dorn and Dickie forward and out of the hotel.

It was over—just like that.

WE ALL THREE sat down limply. We were still limp a few minutes later when Iris came into the vestibule. She had her skis and her light-brown bamboo ski poles over her shoulder. She was humming a bright little tune. She came up to me, smiled affably, and said, "Won't you introduce me to your friends?"

I was still too dazed to think. I made mumbled introductions. Iris nodded to Huysmans and took Juliana's hand. "So pleased to meet you, Miss Guilder. My husband has told me so little about you."

Juliana and Huysmans, deprived of their diamonds, were too dejected to react.

Iris said, "I just saw a lot of customs men, darling. What were they doing?"

"Arresting Dorn and Dickie for Anstey's murder," I said. "Alessandro was caught in Washington, and broke down. It's absolutely crazy. The maddest coincidence. I don't understand ..."

Iris sat down, propping her skis and poles against a pillar. She looked very lovely and very solemn. "It's not exactly a coincidence. I kind of figured it would come through about now."

I stared. I said, "What in heaven's name ... ?"

"It was quite simple really," said Iris. "I thought about it yesterday while you were asleep. After all, we knew Alessandro was going to be hanging around the Sherry-Carlton in Washington, waiting for you."

"Yes, but ..."

"So I called the New York police. Anonymously. It's surprising how charming they are to anonymous voices. I told them if they wanted to get a slant on the Anstey–Purvis murders to arrest an Italian called Alessandro at the Sherry-Carlton in Washington. I gave a description. I then said they could probably get him to confess if they told him that his confederates—Stephen Dorn and Dickie—had just been arrested on the Ski-Monarch. I told them to tell Alessandro that Dorn and Dickie had turned state's evidence against him. I told them that when Alessandro broke down they'd be able to have Dorn and Dickie arrested up here. I told them about Dorn's scar, so's they could identify him. Apparently it all worked out all right."

She looked at me placidly. "After all, fun's fun. And it was all right haring up here in the ski-train. But I thought it would be more comfortable for you if they *were* arrested for the murders in the end."

I stared at her. She'd saved my life in the craziest possible way. And now, by an even crazier way, she'd managed to have Dorn and Dickie arrested by remote control at the most crucial moment. Someone, I thought, should put up a monument.

Huysmans and Juliana were staring at her. She was as entirely unruffled as ever.

"Now, Peter, I've been dying to hear what it's all about. What was this transfer? And how are Mr. Huysmans and Miss Guilder involved?"

I stared again. I blurted, "You—you mean you don't know?"

"Of course I don't know. How have I had a chance? At Grand Central I managed to locate Dickie. It was the sheerest accident. He was in the crowd ahead of me and I heard him saying, 'It's no use waiting to hear from Alessandro.' So I clung to him. Then I saw you'd been smart enough to pick up Dorn. But I never knew what it was all about. No one would ever tell me a thing."

Skiers, attracted by news of the customs men and their arrest, were streaming into the vestibule. I said, "Let's all get back to that drawing-room."

We did. Iris followed patiently with her skis and ski poles.

I told her everything then, every darn' foolish thing I had done, the story Huysmans and Juliana had given me—everything. Juliana joined in, too.

When we'd finished Iris looked at Juliana. "So it really was as big as that. Diamonds that belong to the Dutch government?"

Juliana nodded miserably. "You can't imagine what a blow this is for us, Mrs. Duluth. We've been working night and day; we've had only that one desperate hope that we'd be able to get them back. And now, at the last minute, everything seems to have slipped out of our fingers."

IRIS TOSSED BACK her dark hair. "And you didn't really want to bring in the police? You say they would have delayed everything. And your country needs the diamonds right away—needs the money?"

Juliana nodded.

Iris looked thoughtful for a moment. Then she said, "Bali's Dutch, isn't it? I've always wanted to go there. It would be a shame not to have it properly defended." She got up slowly and, crossing to her skis, picked up one of the bamboo poles. "Queen Wilhelmina's kind of sweet, too."

While we three stared blankly, she started unscrewing the end of one of the poles. It came off. She shook the pole. Fantastically, like something out of the *Arabian Nights*, diamonds started pouring out of the hollow bamboo, sparkling and glistening on the pretentious Turkish carpet. I'd never known so many diamonds existed.

Juliana gave a little scream. Huysmans rose unsteadily.

Iris went on pouring. She looked up. "There are just as many in the other one," she said. "Of course, if I'd known the police were going to arrest Dorn and Dickie, I wouldn't have snitched the poles. But, since I did snitch them, I leave it up to you. Tell the police; don't tell the police; pay them a conscience-money check for the customs amount; do what you think's best."

I was asleep. That's what it was. I was asleep and dreaming. "But, Iris, how … ?"

She blinked. "Really, darling, nothing could have been easier. Didn't you notice Dickie's poles? His and Dorn's were black hickory when they started out for the Ramp, and Dickie's were brown bamboo when they came back. I noticed them immediately. Since I knew someone was going to get something from somewhere, and since the whole thing was tied up with skiing, anyway, I knew what we wanted had to be in them."

Black hickory—brown bamboo. Vaguely I had noticed. But I'd been too dumb to realize its significance.

"I had to get them," said Iris, "so I knocked Dickie down on the ski-slope and managed to grab his poles instead of mine in the tangle. I suppose it was crazy. He was after me and he'd probably have caught up with me if they hadn't arrested him. But"—she shrugged—"no one else was doing anything, so I thought it was up to me."

JULIANA AND HUYSMANS were gazing hypnotized at the diamonds. I was gazing hypnotized at Iris. All this—and she was so beautiful, too!

I said, "Darling, I don't believe in you. You're not real. You're just too—too damn' resourceful."

She grimaced. "There's nothing a girl won't do for the man of her choice."

Huysmans had turned to her. His lips were trembling. "Mrs. Duluth, I don't know … I can't say …"

"Don't be silly," said Iris. "I didn't do anything. Only messed things up. You'd have gotten your diamonds, anyway."

"But—but this facilitates … With the diamonds actually in my possession, it will be so much easier with the authorities. It … Mrs. Duluth, isn't there some way I can show my gratitude?"

"Certainly not." Iris looked righteous. "You gave my husband a ten-thousand-dollar check, and we tore it up. There's an old family motto: No Duluth takes money he hasn't earned."

"Nonsense!" said Huysmans. "Nonsense! I would have had to pay Anstey that much, and more, for the information your husband brought me. And talking about not having earned it … I insist. I shall write another check immediately."

He started fumbling out his checkbook, and began to scribble at a desk. Iris looked at him. She looked at the diamonds. She looked at me.

"Well," she stammered, "if—if you insist …" And then: "And since my husband's rather impractical—perhaps it would be wiser to make it out to me."

She turned to me. She took my arms. She looked impossibly beautiful.

"Hot dog!" she breathed. "Hot *diggity* dog!"

Murder with Flowers

Iris and I were dancing at the Opal Room. A rumba orchestra was doing wicked things. We were very groomed and expensive and chic that night. Very gay, too. Because it was our first wedding anniversary and we were pleased about it.

Other people were dancing there, too, I suppose. I didn't notice them, except maybe to feel sorry for them for not having Iris. Iris was wonderful. Wonderful and dangerous in a gown that didn't cover much territory above the hips. I tried to decide if any other woman had ever been so glamorous. I thought it unlikely.

"Darling," she said, "we do a mean rumba, don't we?"

"Yes, darling," I said. "We do."

"Mr. and Mrs. Peter Duluth!" she said. "Twelve months later, and it still sounds—voluptuous!"

It was then that we saw the Black Beard.

He was sitting alone at a table close to the dance floor. A massive, imperial gentleman, immaculately black and white, with a white carnation in his lapel. His beard sprouted magnificently—jet-black and godlike.

There was an empty champagne bottle at his side. It didn't look as if it was the first empty champagne bottle that had been there that evening. He was gazing at it and weaving slightly in his chair.

We were only a couple of feet away when he looked up from the champagne bottle and saw us. At least, it was Iris he saw. Naturally. Somewhere, above the beard, his eyes lit up. The beard waggled in a roguish, satyr smile. One heavy lid lowered at Iris in a ponderous wink.

THEN SUDDENLY, as he really focused on her, his face went blank. And another expression came—a kind of shocked amazement, that was almost horror. "You ... !" he said.

He tried to get up, sank back, and then did get up. He leaned across the table toward us. Very slowly, he said,

"I warned you. On page eighty-four I warned you. Are you mad being out tonight—of all nights—with your picture all over *The Onlooker?*"

That was an odd thing for a complete stranger to say. But I didn't rumba Iris away. Something kept us there. I think it was the Ancient Mariner quality of the black beard and the steady, unwavering stare.

He swayed slightly. The black beard bobbed in a refined little hiccup.

"The white rose!" he said. "And—the—red—rose ... !" And then, emphatically: "They mean blood...."

He stopped. I pushed Iris backward and then sideways. Fantastically, I was a little scared. I don't think Iris was. I think she was just curious.

The music went: Pomp-tipomptipom—*pom*-pom. The Beard was still staring at Iris.

She smiled suddenly and said, "Go on. The white rose and the red rose ... What about them?"

"The white rose—and the red rose. They're out. You know they're out."

He raised one of the large hands. The gesture practically toppled him forward into the champagne bottle. Pointing a weighty, ambassadorial finger, he said, "It's life or death for you, young lady. You must realize that." He paused. "The elephant hasn't forgotten. Never ... the elephant. Life or death."

THE MUSIC WAS throbbing. All around us sleek, expensive people were dancing sleekly and expensively. He was only an old drunk with a black beard. There was nothing to be alarmed about.

And yet ...

"Life or death," he said. "You mustn't die, young lady. You are too beautiful to die."

Slowly, like a hillside settling down after an earth tremor, he sank back into his chair. His eyes went far away and sad. He hiccuped again—daintily. He had obviously forgotten us.

No one around seemed to have noticed anything. The music was seething. I started pushing Iris away from the man.

We were 'way over the other side of the floor when I said, "Is that Beard a part of your past, darling?"

"I—I never even *saw* him before." There was a shaken look in her eyes. "Life or death! Why should the white rose and the red rose mean blood—for me?"

"Just drunken nonsense," I said.

"He said my picture was in *The Onlooker*. It isn't in *The Onlooker*, Peter. Or is it?"

"I don't know," I said.

We neither of us read *The Onlooker*. But millions of other people do. It tells you all about everything so snappily.

We pretended we had lost interest then. We went on acting like two elegant people being gay on their wedding anniversary. But it was all rather synthetic.

Suddenly Iris said, "After all, Peter, you're a famous play producer and I'm a sort of actress. Maybe I *am* in *The Onlooker*."

"Maybe."

"Let's—let's buy a copy."

"Yes. Let's."

We scuttled off the dance floor. That showed just how skin-deep our indifference was.

THE OPAL ROOM is part of the ultra-swank St. Anton Hotel. We hurried through the tables with the music tom-tomming behind us. We were out in corridors with inch-thick carpets and enormous mirrors. We reached a sort of central lounge which housed a magazine stand.

We went to the stand. Everyone turned and stared at Iris. They always do—especially after midnight. One man stared in particular. He was thin and sharp-nosed and youngish in a gray trench coat with a light gray hat. I noticed him vaguely because he was biting his nails. Biting them savagely and looking at Iris, with something nasty about his mouth.

At the stand I said, "*The Onlooker*, please," to a depressed blonde.

She gave it to me. Iris snatched it and started leafing through the pages. I stood at her side.

Two women with exotic perfumes swished by, patting their necks. The man in the gray trench coat stood there nibbling at his nails and watching Iris sidelong behind a cigarette.

"*Farming*," read Iris. "*Sports* … female discus-throwing champion … that's not me … *Theater* … Circus opens at Lawrence Stadium tomorrow … No … *Art* … Oh, look, Peter!"

I was looking, all right. It was uncanny. There under the heading *Art* was a photograph. It was a photograph of a very beautiful woman, a woman whom anyone except a husband could easily have taken for Iris. Dark, with those same amazing eyes, that devastating bone structure.

Under the photograph it said: *Eulalia Crawford*. And under that: *She does everything except stick pins in them.*

"Eulalia Crawford!" said Iris.

"She's a dead ringer for you."

"Nonsense." Iris looked ominous. "She's at least ten years older."

"Not to a drunken Beard in a dim light," I said, trying to wriggle out of that. "It's obvious he mistook you for her."

We read what it said about Eulalia Crawford. It didn't help much. It told us that Eulalia Crawford was a "pulchritudinous, toothsome" dollmaker. She had a studio downtown. She made the smartest portrait dolls for the smartest people. In fact, after a modest beginning designing carnival figures, she had lifted the doll business into the realms of art. "I do everything with dolls," she had told the reporter laughingly, "except stick pins in them."

"Eulalia Crawford, the dollmaker!" said Iris. "Peter, I've—I've heard of her. She—she's a sort of a relative."

"A relative?"

"Yes." Iris looked excited. "A fifth cousin, or something like that."

"It explains why you look alike," I said. "But that's all it explains."

"But she's in danger—terrible danger," said Iris slowly. "I could tell he meant it, Peter—the Beard. I could tell from his face. He really knows there's danger for her. The red rose—the white rose—life or death."

WE STOOD THERE in that elegant lounge. From somewhere far off the rumba sidled through to us, a torrid echo of the South. I looked up. I caught the eye of the man in the gray trench coat. He glanced away.

"If there's danger for Eulalia," said Iris suddenly, "we must warn her."

"Warn her?"

"Yes." Iris looked beautiful and purposeful. "After all, she's blood of my blood and ..."

"But just because a crazy, drunken Beard ..."

"He wasn't a crazy Beard. He was very sane."

"Then, if you think so, go back and get the truth out of him."

She shook her head. "He'd be suspicious once he knew I wasn't Eulalia. And if I was Eulalia he'd know I wouldn't have to ask him the truth. I must telephone Eulalia."

It sounded silly to me. But Iris said something else stubborn about blood of her blood. Iris is very New England about family responsibilities.

"But—but what will you say?" I asked.

"Tell her about the Beard and the red rose and the white rose and page eighty-four and the elephant." Iris looked calm.

She started toward a lighted sign saying *Telephones*. I sighed and followed. As I did so, I happened to glance over my shoulder, and I noticed that the man in the gray trench coat was strolling, very casually, after us. I wasn't worried, but I was curious.

IRIS REACHED THE Manhattan phone book ahead of me. Efficiently, she started turning pages, murmuring, "Crawford,

Eulalia … Crawford, Eulalia … Here she is." She disappeared into a phone booth. The man in the trench coat loitered aimlessly. Soon Iris came out again. There was a "Marines-to-the-rescue" gleam in her eyes.

"Cousin Eulalia" —I liked that "Cousin!" — "wasn't there, Peter. But she's expected any minute. A man answered, a man with a stammer."

"A stammer?"

"Yes. A stammer. He said it would be fine for us to go down right away."

I stared. "You mean we're going to Eulalia *now?*"

"Of course, darling." She looked dreamy and thrilled to the bone. "We've wined and dined and danced, Peter. Now we plunge into a romantic adventure. Cousins, black beards, and roses! What could be gayer?" She paused. "This," she said, meaning it, "is exactly my idea of how to celebrate our first anniversary."

I had a strong feeling that I didn't agree.

The man with the gray trench coat seemed to have lost interest. I saw him ahead of us, moving away down the lounge toward the main door of the hotel. I went back to the Opal Room and paid my check. I peered through the dancers, looking for the wretched Beard who had started the trouble. I couldn't see him.

When I got back to Iris, she had unchecked her silver fox cap? and had it over her shoulders. She looked exactly the way a girl in a silver fox cape should look—slender and beautiful and distinguished, and good enough to eat. We started toward the swinging doors leading to the street.

Iris said, "You noticed that man in the gray trench coat, Peter? I—I didn't like him." Her expression was rather odd. "The way he looked at me. Almost as if he knew me and …"

"And what?"

But she didn't say any more about it, because at that moment we got tangled up with a large, liveried doorman who started calling us a taxi. We got into it and I gave Eulalia Crawford's address.

It was raining—a slight drizzle spattering the windows of the taxi. Iris seemed remote, her thoughts like a thin layer of cellophane between us. Once she turned to look out of the rear window. She didn't say anything. Then, later, as we swung off Fifth Avenue somewhere in the teen streets, she turned around again.

Softly she said, "I may be crazy, Peter. But I think we're being followed. Look."

I scrambled around and stared out through the rear window. I could see the bright headlights of a private automobile. It was just swinging off Fifth Avenue behind us.

"It's been there ever since we left the St. Anton," said Iris.

I said suddenly, "Do we have to go through with this screwball idea?"

"It's such a heavenly screwball idea," said Iris. "And if someone *is* following us ..."

"What?"

"Then it probably means the whole thing is serious. All the more reason to warn Eulalia."

THE TAXI WAS crawling now in a dimly lit, deserted side street. The driver was peering out of his window at the house numbers. The other car was still behind us.

"Two-thirty-five," said the driver. "Here we are."

He had stopped in front of a house. There were lighted windows in it, and the door, white-painted, showed a brightly illuminated hallway. I paid the fare and we stepped out. The taxi drove off.

And then it all happened, like something in one of those artificially speeded-up movies.

The car which had been dawdling behind us suddenly accelerated and came roaring forward. We swung around. We stood there by the curb, hypnotized for a moment, watching the car zoom through the dead, dark street toward us.

And as we watched it, something hurtled out of it—something large and red, soaring through the air and splashing on the damp sidewalk at our feet. We both stared down at it. I felt a kind of amazement, teetering over into horror. Because the thing was a bouquet of roses—deep scarlet roses.

I was still staring stupidly at the roses when Iris gave a little cry, grabbed at my arm, and said, "Duck, Peter!"

I followed her lead, half collapsing to the sidewalk. Only just in time …

A split second later the sharp report of a gun snarled, once and then again. I heard bullets, whistling close to my ear.

"The door!" shouted Iris. "Get to the door!"

Quicker than seemed humanly possible, we both half ran, half scrambled to the outer, glass-paneled door of two-thirty-five. I tugged the door open and pushed Iris in. I dashed in behind her, slamming the door.

The second inner door was locked. We were trapped there in the little hallway. Outside in the street I could hear the car engine roaring at a standstill. What was to prevent the gunman getting out of the car and coming here?

I looked around wildly at the buzzers. I saw Eulalia Crawford's name coupled with another woman's name. I made a stab at the buzzer. I hit the wrong one.

I stared dazedly. The car engine was still roaring outside. Then an answering buzz sounded in the inner door. Like a flash Iris pushed the door inward. I didn't know what was going on in the street any more. I think I heard the car drive away. But I didn't care. I slammed the door behind us.

"Eulalia's studio," panted Iris. "The man on the phone said it was on the top floor."

WE STARTED TUMBLING up the stairs. What sort of a wedding anniversary was this turning out to be?

Iris said breathlessly, "Did you see the man who shot at us?"

I hadn't. I said so. "But you did?"

She nodded. "I saw him. Peter, he was wearing a gray trench coat and a gray hat. He was the man who bit his nails. The man who was in the vestibule of the St. Anton."

That was a shock, and yet suddenly it gave a sort of sense to the fantastic thing that had happened.

"The man from the St. Anton," repeated Iris. "And the bouquet of red roses ... The red rose—and the white rose."

We had reached the top floor but one, and were hurrying down a dimly lit hallway, when a door opened and a woman in a pink wrapper peered out. In an uneasy moment I realized she was the woman who's buzzer I had pressed by mistake. I muttered, "Sorry. A mistake. We want Miss Crawford."

She slammed her door shut.

I joined Iris on the top landing. There was only one apartment up there. Its door had the elegantly painted legend: *Eulalia Crawford, Dolls, Inc.* Outside the door, propped against the wall, was a dainty red cellophane umbrella. There was a small puddle of water on the linoleum beneath it.

"See! Her umbrella's still dripping, Peter. That means she hasn't been in long."

Iris looked radiant now. Her finger went forward to press the little buzzer in the door-frame. Shaken as I was, seeing her do that made me sensible again.

"Stop!" I said. "Don't press the buzzer."

Her hand remained poised. "Why ever not, Peter?"

"You've got to be sensible. The man at the St. Anton, he—he mistook you for Eulalia Crawford, the way the Beard did. He saw you reading *The Onlooker*. He followed us to this house. He was sure then—so he shot at you. He tried to kill you because he thought you were Eulalia."

"Bright boy," said Iris. "Go to the head of the class." Her hand moved slowly toward the buzzer.

"Don't, Iris. I'm not going to let you get into this any deeper."

"Nonsense." Iris looked determined. "Eulalia's the only one who can explain. And if you think I'm going through life never knowing why I was shot at you're crazy."

She rang the buzzer then, imperiously. We waited, but there was no reply.

"That's funny."

She rang again. After the drone of the buzzer stopped, a deep silence enveloped the top floor of two-thirty-five.

Iris stooped down then, so that she could see under the door. "The lights are on inside, Peter. And the umbrella's dripping. She *must* be in."

Her hand slipped to the doorknob. She turned it and, surprisingly, the door opened.

Iris stepped into the little hall. This was mad, crazy.... I followed her, closing the door behind us.

It was an ordinary little hall. But I didn't like the silence. I don't quite know why. Possibly because, if Eulalia was there, she had no right to be so quiet. Ahead of us was the main room, the studio.

We could see only part of it, through the archway leading from the hall. But it was rather a weird sight—because of the dolls. There were dozens of them, sprawled over everything—life-size dolls, middling-size dolls, small dolls, dolls of women in evening gowns and men in tuxedos, dolls of different nationalities, dolls of clowns, ballet dancers, trapeze artists in tights—every sort of doll. And somehow they were sinister.

Iris was almost on the threshold of the studio. Softly she called, "Miss Crawford."

I tautened. Nothing happened.

Iris stepped into the studio. She made a sound—a sharp, choking sound.

"Iris! What is it? What ...?"

I ran to join her. The swarm of dolls stared from their dozens of baleful, sightless eyes. All through those awful moments, I was conscious of them as a sort of horror background. But they were only a background. Because I saw at once what Iris had seen. Part of the studio had not been visible from the hall. It was visible now, all right.

THERE WAS A DESK—a large, modernistic desk. It was, inevitably, strewn with dolls, little dolls. But it wasn't the dolls. In a chair in front of the desk was a woman. She was wearing a lemon-yellow evening gown. I couldn't see her face, because she was slumped forward, the little dolls clustering around her. But I could see her back. And I could see the knife plunged deep into the flesh between the shoulder blades.

"Peter—is—is she dead?" Iris ran toward the woman, her hand going out.

"Don't touch her, Iris!"

I was at her side. I was looking down at the woman's face. It was in profile, resting on her hands, gazing pointlessly at a little overturned doll of a blond woman in spangled tights. That was really the worst moment.

"Eulalia!" breathed Iris.

But I could only think—Iris. In those awful seconds the resemblance was like a blow on the mouth. Eulalia Crawford was older, yes. But she was terrifyingly like Iris—the hair, the lovely, serene profile, the way the cheekbones curved.

My thoughts were reeling. Just a few moments before, Iris had been shot at. Why? Because she was mistaken for Eulalia Crawford. That's what I had thought. But ... what about this? Hadn't Eulalia been dead—even then when the bouquet of red roses was hurled at us from the car?

Iris's voice came dimly: "Peter, the—the man who answered the phone. The man with the stammer. He must have murdered her. He urged me to come. He left the door open so we could get in. Because he wanted us to get in; he wanted people to think that we ..." She had moved around the desk. Sharply she called, "Look! Peter—look!"

I joined her, numbly. She was pointing.

There behind the desk, strewn haphazard across the carpet in a sort of nightmare canopy, were dozens of roses. But this time the roses were not red. They were white.

Iris's hand went down to the desk, supporting her. There was a blue book lying there with gold lettering. She touched it, and it moved, revealing something beneath it—a piece of paper with writing on it.

Iris picked it up and stared at it. "Peter, she—she must have been writing this when it happened."

Quaveringly, she started to read it aloud:

"Dear Lina:
"I have to write to you to warn you. Because there's danger—mortal danger. The white rose—and the red rose—"

Iris looked up. "There's more. But I—I can't read it." She paused. "Lina! Eulalia—and now Lina, too." She was very pale. Suddenly she said, "Peter, what are we going to do?"

WHAT, INDEED? CALL the police? That was the normal thing to do when you discovered a body. But could we call the police? What could we say? We had broken into a strange woman's apartment. Why? Because of the red rose and the white rose. What were the red rose and the white rose? We didn't know. Who had told us about them? A drunken black-beard. Who was the drunken black-beard? We didn't know. Where could we find him to check our story? We didn't know. Why hadn't we, a reputable play producer and his reputable wife, called the police in the first place if we thought something criminal was afoot? We didn't know. At least, we did know. It was our wedding anniversary and we thought we'd have some fun. Fun!

The whole madhouse tale scuttled through my thoughts. Who on earth would believe that? Certainly not the hard-headed police.

I glanced at the front door. The sight of it decided me. It seemed to decide Iris, too. Almost simultaneously we said, "Come on. Let's get out of here."

Together we ran to the front door. Iris's hand went forward for the knob.

It was then that we heard the scratch of a key in the lock outside.

Wildly I thought, "That other name by the buzzer—Eulalia's roommate!"

The door was pushed open inward. And a woman stood there. I shall never have more than the vaguest impression of that woman. A youngish woman with very blond hair and very red lips.

She was just as startled as we. She came toward us, staring. Every possible sign of guilt must have been scrawled across our faces. Eulalia's roommate went on staring. "Who—who are you?"

Who were we! We stood there, stiff and lifeless as the dolls.

"What are you doing here?"

Then her eyes left us. She gazed into the room beyond. I saw the horror coming into her face. And then she screamed. "Eulalia!" And, with a rising hysterical crescendo, "You killed her! You murdered her!"

After that she wasn't saying any actual words. It was just a long, animal scream.

We were beyond any reasonable process of thought then. The woman's blind terror infected us, too. With amazing teamwork born of panic, Iris and I dashed toward the woman, pushed her aside, and bolted along the landing outside to the stairs. In a split second we were stumbling downward.

And then we were out on the dark street, out in the drizzle—running. And, miraculously, there was a taxi. I hailed it. By a supreme effort we managed to change ourselves into a languid couple in evening dress who nonchalantly needed a taxi.

"Where to?" said the driver.

"Where to?" echoed Iris. "Oh—uptown. Somewhere gay and expensive. The Continental, I think. Yes, the Continental."

That was smart of her. I would have given our home address. Now that we were fugitives from justice that might well have been fatal.

After the horror of two-thirty-five, the impeachably upper-crust atmosphere of the Continental was soothing. We were taken to a table. The lights were dim and the orchestra was playing a dreamy waltz. Everyone was dancing. Dancing seemed a very sensible thing to do. We danced.

I loved it—having Iris close in my arms. For a few misguided moments I really started thinking this was a nice wedding anniversary, after all. Then, inevitably, Iris brought us back to reality.

"Running out like that!" she said softly. "We were crazy, Peter. We lost our nerve."

She was so soft and warm in my arms. "Yes," I said. "We did."

"That girl who broke in on us, that roommate of Eulalia's," said Iris. "Of course, she thinks we killed Eulalia."

"Yes," I said dreamily. Iris waltzes divinely.

"And when the police come, she'll be able to give them a perfect description of us. So will the woman whose buzzer we rang. And the two taxi drivers—the one who took us there and the one who brought us here. It oughtn't to be hard for the police to catch up with us."

"True."

SUDDENLY I DIDN'T want to dance any more. I wanted a drink. We had the waiter bring highballs to our table. Mine didn't help my mood any. Iris's romantic adventure!

Iris was clasping her drink in both hands, looking ethereal. Slowly she said, "You know, Peter, we've done everything but confess to that murder."

"Exactly."

"Probably the police are after us even now. And it's not only that. The man with the gray trench coat shot at us once. Maybe he wants to shoot at us again."

"Goody," I said dourly.

"And I don't see how we can possibly exonerate ourselves unless …"

"Unless—what?"

"Unless we find out the truth. I mean the truth about the red roses and the white roses. Then we could go to the police and make a clean breast of it."

"And how could we find out the truth?"

"I don't know." Iris thought, and then opened her pocket-book. "Maybe this! This letter Eulalia had started to write."

She pulled it out and handed it to me.

I groaned. "So you stole valuable evidence, too! That's another ten years on our sentence."

"I'm sorry, darling." Iris looked rueful. "I just forgot to put it down."

I stared with a jaundiced eye at the brief, cryptic scrawl: "Dear Lina:

"I have to write to you to warn you ..."

Iris leaned over and looked, too. "We know that—about warning Lina of the red rose and the white rose. But that other line I couldn't read. Can you make it out?"

I stared at the sprawling, indecipherable script. " 'The white rose and the red rose are out,' " I read. " 'And the something' ... 'The—the crocus is opening.' "

The note broke off there. We stared at each other. "The crocus!" exclaimed Iris. "The red rose—the white rose—the opening crocus ..."

"The whole damn' botanical garden."

"Lina would know," said Iris. "There's danger for her—just the way there was danger for Eulalia. Lina would be able to tell us everything."

"Lina—U. S. A.," I said. "She's going to be a cinch to locate."

IRIS WASN'T LISTENING. Suddenly her eyes lit up. "The Beard!" she exclaimed.

"To hell with the Beard," I said.

"But, Peter, the Beard knows everything. *He* could prove our story was really on the level. If we took the Beard to the police, everything—everything might be all right."

"I might remind you that we don't know the Beard's name. We don't know where he lives or what—"

"That doesn't matter." Iris was her old, enthusiastic self again. "There aren't so many black beards in New York."

She rose, wrapping her silver fox around her. "Come on. We're going to find the Beard."

Five minutes later we were in a taxi driving back to the St. Anton. I was sure the Beard wouldn't be there any more. But Iris was bubbling over with hope again.

He wasn't at the Opal Room, of course. We weaved through the tables, fine-combing the guests. Then we divided forces and started excavating the lounges. I had no success. I was returning empty-handed to the main vestibule when Iris came running radiantly toward me.

"The doorman!" she exclaimed. "He's a lovely doorman. He got the Beard a taxi about an hour ago. And he heard him tell the driver to go to the Gray Goose."

The Gray Goose was a halfway fashionable night club in the Fifties. We bundled ourselves into yet another taxi and dashed to the Gray Goose.

We didn't check our coats. We went straight into the ballroom. Two pianos were playing boogie-woogie. A few couples were dancing; but most of them were snuggled up in booths. We started pushing into booth after booth, systematically, peering. And in the last booth we found him.

He was more majestic even than my memory of him. Words could not do justice to the splendors of his beard.

"Hello," said Iris.

Slowly, little by little, he moved his head. Slowly his eyes lit up in a wicked, goatish leer. "Buriful girl," he said.

Iris slipped into the booth, sitting down across from him. I squeezed in after her. She leaned forward, saying urgently, "You remember me, don't you? The Opal Room. You mistook me for Eulalia Crawford."

"Y're not Eulalia Cr'wford." Somewhere beneath the beard that goatish smile had gotten to his mouth. "Much more buriful th'n Eulalia. Younger. Much more buriful." His great hand unfolded from the stem of his champagne glass, groped forward, and fell—flop—on Iris's. "Buriful girl."

Such superb drunkenness seemed to non-plus even Iris. "You must remember me," she said rather lamely. "You told me about the white rose and the red rose."

The Beard's hand left Iris's. He giggled. Then, suddenly, he brandished his arm at a hovering waiter. "Drink!" he said. "Drink for the buriful girl. Champagne."

As the waiter slipped away, the Beard's aimless gaze settled for the first time on me. "Who'sh tha'?" he demanded.

"He's—he's just with me," said Iris.

The Beard came closer and closer. It was almost in my mouth. Above it, his eyes, screwed up around the corners in a fury of concentration, examined my face. "Nasty man," he said. "Nasty man. Go away. Go away." The beard bobbed up and then down. "Boo-oo!"

That was startling, to say the least. Iris was looking rather wild-eyed now. She said desperately, "You've *got* to understand. Please. This is terribly important for us. It's—it's life or death. The elephant never forgets. You mustn't forget. Page eighty-four. You've got to help us."

"Nasty man! Buriful girl." The Beard sank back into his red leather corner. "Tell that man—go away. Won't have him here. *My* booth!"

Iris gave a rather sickly smile. Then she leaned toward me and breathed, "It's no good, darling. He just doesn't like you. But he likes me. Maybe, if you go away, *I* can get something out of him."

Even as she spoke, the Beard's large hand trundled forward and closed again affectionately over hers. He liked *her*, all right!

"Go to the bar," she whispered. "Wait for me there. I'll try and get him to talk."

"But I don't want to leave you with that drunken—"

"Go to the bar, darling."

I went to the bar and, perching myself on a high stool, ordered a highball. I was on my second drink when Iris appeared from the inner room. She was looking a little dazed, but rather triumphant, too.

"What a man!" she said. And then, "But I've got Lina."

"You've got Lina? You mean—you know who she is?"

"No. But I know her name, where she lives. He's canny, Peter, the Beard. Terribly canny. He's not telling a thing. But I tricked that out of him. Because he thinks it's funny. 'Listen,' he said, 'isn't this funny?' And he chanted it."

"Chanted what?"

"Lina Oliver Wendell *Holmes* Brown. Sixteen-seventeen, Smith Street, Brooklyn."

Iris chanted it, too. Personally, I thought the Beard was right. It was a riotously funny name. So what?

IRIS WAS LOOKING pale. "I've been thinking, Peter. And—and there's only one thing to do. The Beard is hopeless until he sobers up. Now, Lina ..."

"Lina?"

"Lina knows the whole story. This thing that happened to Eulalia—I think it's going to happen to Lina."

"Of course it is," I said savagely. "She's got the red rose and the white rose *and* the crocus after her. And, so far as I care, they can all catch up with her and—"

"No, darling. They mustn't catch up with her. Don't you see? Time's everything. Maybe we can still warn Lina in time. And, if we warn her, then she'll have to tell us the truth and—and that's the only way we can get out of this—this jam."

I was beginning to see. "You want us to go to Lina now?" I glanced at my watch. "Now—at two-forty-five A. M."

"Oh, I know it's crazy. Everything's crazy." Iris's lips were trembling. "But, darling—please go to Lina now."

"Me! You mean ... I have to go alone?"

"Darling, I can't let the Beard get away now. I simply can't. We need him. I've got to cling to him through thick and thin. But you ..."

I finished my drink in one gulp. I didn't want to go to Brooklyn.

"Peter, I know it's late. But here ..." She fumbled in her pocketbook and brought out Eulalia's letter. "If you show her this, she'll know you're on the level. You—you will go, won't you?"

I took the letter. I kissed her. "I'll go."

"Darling!" she smiled. "And, as soon as you're through, go straight back to the apartment. I'll try and get there as soon as possible—with the Beard."

"With the Beard? Do we have to adopt the Beard, too?"

"Of course. Tomorrow morning he'll be sober. Tomorrow morning he'll be worth his weight in roses." Iris was adamant. "Remember, darling. Lina Oliver Wendell *Holmes* Brown ..."

"... sixteen-seventeen. Smith Street. Brooklyn."

"Darling!"

I kissed her again. She was utterly beautiful and magnificent and exciting. And I left her to the tender mercies of the amorous Beard. I've never hated doing anything so much in my life....

Sixteen-seventeen Smith Street was a squat, dirty house in a row of uniformly squat and dirty houses. The Browns, I discovered, lived in the basement. And judging from the lighted window, someone was awake—either Mr. or Mrs. Oliver Wendell Holmes Brown. I located the buzzer and pressed it.

The door was pulled open almost before I'd stopped ringing. The speed of it all startled me. In the obscure light from the hall, I could see the woman who stood there on the threshold only dimly—a dark, fluttering little thing with big, big eyes.

"Oliv—!" She broke off with a birdlike, swooping gesture of her hand. "Oh, I—I thought it was my husband." And then, before I had time to open my mouth, she was explaining nervously, "My husband works late at the restaurant. He—he forgot his key. I was waiting up for him."

WE STOOD THERE in the dark area, watching each other.

"Are you Lina Oliver Wendell Holmes Brown?" I asked.

"Yes, yes."

Thank heavens, Lina was alive, anyway!

"What do you want?" She started a little chirping laugh and then, as if the unconventional hour of my visit suddenly frightened her, she added jerkily, "What do you want—so late at night?"

"I've come for Eulalia Crawford," I said.

"Eulalia!" The words came in a thin little Phoebe-bird peep, and Lina's small hands took wing again. Impulsively one hand alighted on my sleeve. She was pulling me into the hall. She closed the door behind us. She was almost running ahead.

I followed into the living-room. There was too much old-fashioned furniture in it, but it was kind of pathetically neat. There were two framed photographs on the mantel—a photograph of a muscular blonde in tights with a toothy smile, and another photograph of a dark little slip of a thing gleaming with tawdry spangles. That second picture was Lina herself, I could tell. She was older now, though.

She was hovering in front of me, staring. "What is it? Why did Eulalia send you?"

I thought of Eulalia's letter. That was as good an opening gambit as any.

I pulled the crumpled piece of paper from my pocket. Watching her, I held it out. "Eulalia wrote this to you," I said.

She stared at the fantastic note. "The white rose—and the red rose!" She looked up. Her lips were as pale as her cheeks. "The roses ..."

I didn't say anything.

Her tongue came out, wetting her lips. I've never seen such real terror in any human eyes. "The letter isn't finished. It isn't in an envelope. It isn't finished. You—you brought it—" She broke off. "What's happened to Eulalia?" And then, in a small, tortured sob, "She's dead! They killed her!"

How had she guessed that? What was I to say? "Mrs. Brown—"

She stepped back. "They killed Eulalia. And you—you brought this letter to me. *You* brought it!" She was still backing away. "You're one of them. You've come to get me, too. The roses ..."

It was then that the sound of the front door buzzer echoed sharply in the hall. Lina swirled around. "Oliver!"

She dashed away from me, calling her husband's name despairingly. I could hear her little footsteps pattering in the hall. "Oliver!"

I heard the basement front door open.

"Oliver ..."

Lina's voice stopped in a little choking gasp. There was a moment of entire silence. Then another voice sounded, a man's voice—a voice that stammered hesitatingly. It said, "H-hello, Lina, d-darling. I'm sure you're g-glad to s-see me."

The sound of that stammering voice toppled me off whatever solid ground there was left. The stammering voice which had answered Iris over Eulalia's phone, the voice of the man who had murdered Eulalia!

I glanced wildly around the stuffy Victorian room. I took a pointless step toward the hall.

And then, ripping through the silence, two revolver shots sounded in brutal, rapid succession. One ... two ...

The nearness of those two shrill explosions was appalling. The quiet that came after was appalling, too. And then, sprouting out of that quietness like a thin, weak tendril, twined a small wailing sound that shriveled into a hissing sigh. A sigh—then a small, subdued noise of a little body crumpling to the floor.

ALL THAT CAME in a second. I hadn't time even to move a finger before it was over—before I heard the clatter of footsteps running away from the door.

I dashed forward out of the living-room into the hall. I knew what I was going to see, of course.

Lina was there, tumbled in a little limp heap by the open front door. There was blood. But it wasn't the blood that was the worst. Thrown over the little prostrate body, like a bizarre funeral canopy, were roses—dozens of pure white roses. Some of the petals weren't white any more. They were a vivid scarlet where the blood had splashed them. I dropped to my knees, bending dazedly over Lina. The red rose and the white rose—they mean blood!

Vaguely, as I knelt there by the night's second corpse, I realized I could still hear the running footsteps of the murderer growing fainter on the dark street outside. Blindly obedient to impulse, I jumped up and ran out. I clambered up the iron stairs to the street and stood there at their head.

I could just see the man. He was running to a parked car. I could make him out, a thin, tall figure. I had been thinking, instinctively, in terms of the man with the gray trench coat, who bit his nails. But, as he reached the car, I caught a glimpse of his profile in the light from a street lamp. It was gaunt and angular, but it wasn't the same profile. He wasn't wearing a trench coat, either. And the most arresting thing about that fleeing figure was his hair. For it was a vivid, gleaming white.

So there were two men with guns abroad that night!

Long before I could have done anything to stop it, the murder car sprang forward and roared away out of sight. I stood there at the head of the iron stairs, trembling under the delayed impact of shock.

The gunfire had not shaken Brooklyn out of its small-hours' sleep. Probably the cavernous pit of the basement had muffled the reports. In any case, the alarm had not as yet been sounded. But soon Oliver Wendell Holmes Brown himself would return from the restaurant. Soon the night would be full of the cry of "Murder."

That brought me back to thinking violently about myself. Here I was hopelessly committed to this second corpse—I, Peter Duluth, the man who, almost certainly, was under suspicion of one murder already.

There was only one possible thing to do next. Poor Lina was dead, her secret still undisclosed. There was nothing I could do for her. So long as I stayed there I was jeopardizing my entire future and Iris's.

Get away, Peter Duluth. Get away—now. Scram!

I made my second major retreat that night. I walked out on Oliver Wendell Holmes Brown, the waiter or whatever he was. I left him to face his tragic homecoming—alone....

WHEN I LET myself into our apartment, it was in total darkness. Iris wasn't there. I turned on all the lights, hating Iris's not being there. It was half past four. Surely all the night clubs were closed by now. I mixed myself a drink and gulped at it while I paced up and down the room. I was full of forebodings. Iris had already been shot at that night. And the Beard—we knew nothing about him. Why had we assumed so readily that he was a friend? For all we knew, he was one of the gang. Why had I left Iris to cope with him alone?

I worked myself up into a frenzy of nerves. I'd never felt so helpless.

And then, about half an hour later, I heard the incalculably sweet sound of her key scratching the front door lock. I ran out into the hall just as the door opened. And she was there. Iris was there.

She stepped into the apartment and then turned back to the corridor, crooning, "Come on, Pussy. This way, Pussy."

I started toward her, saying, "Iris ..." Then I stopped dead in my tracks.

Slowly progressing into the room was a large, ponderous figure in black, a figure with the massive dignity of a Supreme Court justice. But, defying all laws of probability, he was moving on all fours. One large hand padded forward and then another, the substantial rump proceeding soberly behind. The solemn face with its majestic black beard looked unutterably out of place when it stared up at me from six inches above the floor.

The Beard navigated the threshold. Iris closed the door behind him. She turned to me. She looked beautiful but frayed.

"Hello, Peter." She indicated the Beard, who was nuzzling like a huge, playful kitten around her skirt. "He's been like this ever since we came out of the elevator. He thinks he's a pussy cat."

I was still suffering from my gnawing anxiety at her absence. "Where—where have you been?"

"Driving up and down Fifth Avenue," said Iris, "looking for Easter Bunnies."

"You can't see Easter Bunnies in September," I said sensibly.

"He can." Iris shot a withering glance at the sportive Beard. "He could see Niagara Falls in Times Square at this point." And then, despairingly: "Peter, *what* shall we do with him?"

"You haven't got anything out of him?"

"Nothing!" Iris wrung her hands. "It's hopeless. I don't even know his name. He—he just says to call him Pussy."

"Pussy!" said the Beard gravely. And started a laborious attempt to sit up on his haunches. Fantastically, although I've never seen a drunker man, he had not lost one particle of his dignity.

I LOOKED AT IRIS over his head. She looked back at me.

"At least I managed to bring him home," she said wearily. And then, thinking about me: "But—but Lina ... Did you see her? Did you get anything?"

"Lina," I said, "is dead."

"Dead!" Iris's lips went pale. "You—you mean you found her dead like—like Eulalia?"

"She was alive when I got there. She was murdered right under my nose."

Iris's eyes were bleak. Very softly she breathed, "And the roses ...?"

"Of course the roses. White roses. Her body was strewn with them."

"Peter!"

The Beard, who had been squatting there imperviously, suddenly sat down on the carpet. Iris and I exchanged a harassed glance.

"We'd better get him on a couch in the living-room," said Iris. "I can't bear this—this weaving around."

Somehow we managed together to propel the Beard to a couch. He seemed to like it. He nestled back and closed his eyes.

"Now," said Iris to me, "tell me everything."

I did. I told her that whole miserable Brooklyn saga. When I had finished, we both turned and stared at the Beard.

"He's—he's our only hope now," breathed Iris. Ponderous lids still hid his eyes. Impulsively Iris bent over him, took his large shoulders and shook him. His eyes popped open. "You've got to listen," said Iris passionately. "Lina's dead. Eulalia's dead. The white rose and the red rose—they've murdered Eulalia Crawford and Lina Oliver Wendell Holmes Brown."

Suddenly the Beard looked very intelligent. His eyes cleared. His beard took upon itself all the gravity in the world. He opened his mouth. We both leaned forward tensely.

"Miaouw!" he said.

He giggled then—a little girlish giggle.

Iris stamped her foot in frustrated despair.

"You've got to help us," she said. "Eulalia and Lina are murdered."

"Eulalia," repeated the Beard slowly. "Lina."

"Yes, yes. Go on. Eulalia, Lina."

The Beard lifted a large hand and started beating solemn, unrhythmical time in the air. "Eulalia, Lina ... Zelide, Edwina," he said. "Eulalia, Lina ... Zelide, Edwina."

Iris glanced at me triumphantly. "Tell us," she said sharply. "Tell us. Who is Zelide? Who—is—Zelide?"

The Beard stared. "A bird," he said.

"A bird!" Iris shrugged hopelessly. "Edwina, then—who is Edwina?"

"'N elephant," said the Beard promptly. Then his eyes shut once more. He started to snore. The drunken oracle had obviously said his last say.

"It's no good, darling," I said.

"But—but it's got to be." Iris swirled round. "I've been with him for hours. That was the only time he answered me. The only time. Peter, we've got to wake him up. We've got to get him sober."

I looked hopelessly at that vast monument to sleep on the couch. I said, "We might try black coffee."

"Coffee—yes." Iris became excited. "We'll make some. Right now."

She hurried, a beautiful, slender figure, into the kitchen. I followed. Cans and percolators and things clattered around, and a few minutes later the coffee was done.

We went into the living-room together, Iris carrying the coffee on the tray as if it were butter on a lordly dish.

"I ..." she began.

Then she stopped. Because the couch where the Beard had been so epically asleep was empty.

Iris put down the coffee. We both started a feverish and unsuccessful search of the apartment, under the piano and everything. We went out into the hall. The front door was open, telling its own story.

"He's—he's gone," wailed Iris.

That was self-evident. The Beard had been far craftier than we had anticipated. He must have pretended to be asleep. And, during the minutes we had spent in the kitchen, he had made his getaway. The priceless bird had flown.

A mean gray stain of dawn was tinging the sky as we went to bed....

THE FIRST THING that swam into my consciousness when I awoke again at some indeterminate daylight hour was the rustle of paper. I opened heavy eyelids. Iris was standing by my bed, fully dressed, crisp as celery, and indomitably beautiful. But I didn't like the way she looked. It made me suddenly awake. She looked pale and ominous. In her hand she was clutching a morning paper.

"Hello, darling," she said brightly.

"The paper," I said. "Does it say anything about us?"

She didn't speak. She sat down by me and spread the paper out in front of me. It was the front page. At the bottom left corner, I saw the headline screaming about the two mysterious murders. I scanned the column below. There was all the stuff you would expect. Two women killed in different parts of the city ... white roses strewn over both. . . . Then there was a paragraph. It read:

> Miss Doris Lomas, Eulalia Crawford's roommate, surprised two suspicious characters red-handed in the apartment when she returned from a dance. Miss Lomas told the police how she opened the front door of the apartment and saw a man and a woman actually bending over the body of Miss Crawford. They fled when they saw her. But she was able to give a detailed description of both of them....

Detailed description was right! Miss Lomas had a very keen eye. There followed a description of Iris and me, exact to the last zipper.

As I read on, distraught, I reached this:

> Mrs. Clarence Stark, who lives in the apartment below, also saw the murder suspects, and her description fits closely with that of Miss Lomas. Already the taxi driver who drove them to Miss Crawford's apartment from the luxurious St. Anton Hotel has been traced. A second taxi is believed to have driven them from the scene of the crime to the Continental. There the trail ends. But the police are sanguine that soon ...

I stopped. I couldn't read any more. Iris's hand slipped into mine.

"The hunt," said Iris, "is up."

It was indeed. Our worst fears had been justified. Now we were officially stamped as probable murderers pursued by the Law.

"We've only got a little time," said Iris. "A very little time. And we've got to do a lot of thinking."

"We needn't bother thinking," I said gloomily. "We can save that for the long evenings in the penitentiary."

Iris looked at me and decided I wasn't being co-operative. She went out, and came back soon with a tray of breakfast. Balancing the tray with one hand, she pushed the paper off my lap onto the floor. Then she put the tray down in front of me. "Zelide," she mused. "The Beard called her a bird. Why a bird? We've got the facts if only we could put them together. The white rose, the red rose, the crocus—Edwina, the elephant."

She broke off with a sudden little cry. Her body had gone tense. She was staring down at something on the carpet. "Peter," she breathed. "The elephant!" Then she plunged onto her knees by the bedside. I heard her fingers rustling the newspaper wildly. "Peter! I think I've got it."

I PUSHED THE breakfast tray aside. I rolled out of bed onto the floor beside her.

"I saw the ad. I never realized." She grabbed my arm and pointed triumphantly at the newspaper. I stared. Staring back at me from a large ad in the paper were three prancing elephants.

"See, Peter? Eulalia's letter to Lina—we read it wrong. Eulalia's writing was so bad. We thought she said, 'The *crocus* is opening.' She didn't. She said 'The *circus* is opening!' "

Above the elephants, in bold, black letters, were the words: THE CIRCUS IS IN TOWN. GALA OPENING TODAY AT THE LAWRENCE STADIUM.

"That's the clue," breathed Iris. "The circus! Why didn't we guess? Edwina, the elephant. And—and Eulalia had those dolls—those clowns, trapeze artists, and things."

"There was a photograph of Lina in Brooklyn," I cut in, remembering. "A photograph of her all dressed in spangles. She must have been with the circus one time."

"So must Eulalia. Carnival dolls! Don't you remember how *The Onlooker* said she'd started her career making carnival dolls? That's the tie-up between them. Now the others ... Zelide. That sounds like a circus name. Zelide—the bird. Zelide ... Oh, look, Peter."

Once again Iris was crouched over the paper. She was pointing at the bottom of the ad. There, listed with the other attractions, was the announcement: *Madame Zelide, World-Famous Aerialist, with her Amazing Bird Ballet.*

"Zelide—the bird!" exclaimed Iris.

We stayed there crouched together on the floor, staring at each other.

"See how it all makes sense now?" cried Iris. "Eulalia and Lina and Zelide—they must all have been together in the circus."

"And Edwina the elephant?"

That didn't faze her. "Eulalia, Lina, Zelide, and this elephant, Edwina, they all ganged up together and did something connected with roses—something that harmed the man who bites his nails and the man who stutters. That happened in the past. And now the two men are having their revenge." She tossed back her lovely dark hair and looked radiant. "We'll be okay now, darling. Zelide will be able to straighten everything out."

I clambered back into bed and started eating my breakfast. But I wasn't given any peace. Iris clambered onto the bed, too, reached over my coffee for the telephone book and started leafing through it madly.

"What you doing?" I said.

"Lawrence Stadium," she muttered. "Lawrence Stadium. ... Here we are." She dialed a number. Then she began chattering excitedly into the phone to several different stadium extensions, asking for Madame Zelide. Her face, which had been alight with hope, went grave. Then she turned to me, whispering, "Zelide's not there."

I dunked toast in my coffee. "Then ask to speak to Edwina, the elephant," I said.

Iris withered me and said into the phone, "Do you know where I could reach Madame Zelide, please? ... Okay.... Thanks."

SHE SLAMMED DOWN the receiver. "Zelide," she said, "is staying at the St. Anton. See how it all ties up?"

"At the St. Anton?"

"That explains what happened to us last night. The two gunmen must have divided up the job. The one who stutters was detailed to get Eulalia and Lina; the one who bites his nails was detailed to get Zelide at the St. Anton. While he was there he saw me, mistook me for Eulalia, figured his buddy had slipped up on the job, so he tried to kill me. That makes sense, doesn't it?"

Iris picked up the telephone again. She dialed.

After a brief talk with someone at the St. Anton she hung up disconsolately. "It's no good, Peter. Zelide went out last night and she hasn't come back yet—or called."

"I thought as much," I said darkly. "Farewell, Zelide— corpse number three."

She laid her head against my shoulder. It was nice, even though it did get in the way of my breakfast. She seemed to be thinking. Finally she looked at her watch. "The circus begins at two."

"So what?"

"So—we go to the circus." Iris pushed herself around so that she was staring vehemently into my face. "That's the only place we can hope to find out anything." She paused. "You never know. Maybe we'll even stumble into the Beard there. Don't they have bearded men in circuses?"

"Bearded ladies, darling," I said. "Maybe that's it. Maybe the Beard is a lady."

Iris patted her hair and looked far away. "The Beard is *not* a lady," she said. "You can take that from me." ...

IT WAS ABOUT one-thirty when we left the apartment. Iris was elaborately glamorous in an outfit which culminated in an exotic Dietrich veil. I, very Palm Beach and groomed, sported a pair of heavy sunglasses. The veil and the sunglasses were a forlorn attempt at disguise. The aggressive chic was intended to disconcert policemen, too; because Iris had the bizarre theory that the more overprivileged you seemed the less criminal you looked.

We made the circus, unmolested. And the moment after I'd bought ringside tickets and we'd joined the festive throng scrambling into the great stadium I felt more secure.

Iris looked at her watch and said, "It's going to start any minute, Peter."

"So—what do we do?"

"Zelide, of course." She looked tense through the veil. "We've got to see if she's come. We've got to warn her before the performance begins."

We both looked around through the crowd. Iris said, "Downstairs to the side shows.... That's the way to get backstage."

We started wriggling and pushing through children. We were running down broad stone stairs. We reached the broad, long basement where the side shows were.

Animals were everywhere; in cages with lurid, jungle backdrops, macaws, flaming scarlet, were screeching. The tallest man in the world was sharing a ham sandwich with a tattooed lady. Strolling toward us, hand in hand, were the fat woman and a little golden-haired midget.

We hurried to the fat woman and the midget. Iris asked urgently, "Where can we find Madame Zelide, please?"

The midget jerked with a tiny thumb over her shoulder. "Dressing-rooms back there, lady. They'll tell you."

We left them and hurried on through the animal cages toward the rear of the basement. There, at the end of the long room, we found ourselves in an insane outcrop of elephants. Elephants were everywhere.

Iris gave a little exclamation, pointed, and breathed, "Peter, look—Edwina!"

I looked, and she was right. The legendary Edwina was quite definitely there. She was in an open stall of her own in regal solitude, a vast brown elephant with tree-trunk legs, vague, kindly eyes, and an immense pink ribbon around her neck. A message hung on the stall said in large letters: *Edwina, the Oldest Elephant in Captivity.*

"Edwina," said Iris in an awed whisper, and fluttered with her hand. "If the Beard's right, Peter, she knows the whole truth about the roses."

Edwina lifted her trunk into a sort of ess-bend, flicked her ears above the pink ribbon, and whistled. And then, from the distant arena, a crash of cymbals blared.

The circus had begun.

I said urgently, "We'd better get to Zelide."

There was an archway ahead. We hurried to it and found ourselves at the mouth of one of the vast entrances to the arena itself. Here there was wild activity as the opening parade started swaying out into the ring.

Iris grabbed a clown. "Zelide?" she said. "Where's Zelide's room?"

The clown pointed backward. "Down the corridor, first to the left, first to the right—the third room."

We scurried on to Zelide's room.

Iris knocked on the closed door. Nothing happened. She knocked again.

"She's not there, Peter. She ..." Impulsively Iris pushed the door inward. I stepped in after her. The room was empty. I closed the door behind us.

THE ROOM WAS tawdry. It smelled of stale make-up. A curtained closet bulged with theatrical costumes. There was a cluttered dressing table. And a mirror above it, encircled with pinned-up photographs.

I went to the dressing table and looked at the photographs. Iris was with me. All the pictures were of the same woman—a blonde with a dazzling smile. They were all signed scrawlingly: *Zelide*. The face was dimly familiar. Then I remembered the photograph at Lina's home.

"We're on the track," I said. "Lina had a photograph of Zelide, at her house."

"And—and the doll at Eulalia's," breathed Iris. "Do you remember the little blond doll in tights that was on the desk by Eulalia's head? That must have been Zelide, too."

We looked at each other.

"What are we going to do, Peter? She isn't here. It's no use staying." Then, desperately, "She can't be dead, too."

She broke off. She was looking down at the dressing table. Balanced precariously between jars of cold cream was a brown-paper package. It had Zelide's name on it and a plastering of stamps. It was marked: URGENT, RUSH, SPECIAL DELIVERY.

Iris and I had the same idea simultaneously. Both our hands went out for that package. I got it first. *Rush, urgent* ... It might be something. It just might.

I started tearing off the wrappings. "It's—it's only a book," I said.

But I went on unwrapping it. And suddenly we saw the book. It came out with the back of the dust cover on top. It consisted of a single, large photograph ... the photograph of a majestic gentleman with a magnificent, sprouting black beard.

"Peter!" exclaimed Iris. "It's the Beard!"

I turned the book over. I looked dazedly at the title. It said: CRIMES OF OUR TIMES. And, underneath, the author's name: EMMANUEL CATT, AMERICA'S MOST DISTINGUISHED CRIMINOLOGIST.

"The Beard!" said Iris again. "The Beard wrote it. And last night he called himself Pussy, because his name's Catt," she added. "Peter, look; there's a note clipped inside. Open the book."

My hand was rather wobbly. As I moved to open the book, I pushed the back dust cover off. It flopped limply. And then I gave a grunt of surprise. The binding under the paper cover was blue—blue with gold lettering. That conjured up sharp memories.

"This book!" I said. "There was a blue book with gold lettering on Eulalia's desk. He must have sent each of them a book."

There was a note clipped onto the flyleaf. It said, in neat, meticulous handwriting: *See page 84.* Just that. *See page 84.*

"Page eighty-four!" exclaimed Iris. "That's what the Beard said to me. 'I warned you on page eighty-four.' "

I leafed shakily through the book, glancing at the chapter headings as the pages flicked by. One chapter would be called: The Mystery of Something or Other, the next the Mystery of Something Else. Suddenly I stopped.

On page 84 began Chapter Eleven. And it was called: *The Mystery of the White Rose and the Red Rose.* Penciled into the top corner were the words: *The Red Rose and The White Rose are out. You must realize your danger, Madame Zelide, E. C.*

"Here!" said Iris, awed. "The solution was here all the time in the book."

"Lina can't have gotten her book," I said, "because she hadn't been warned when I got there."

Tensely we both stared down, reading the first sentence of Chapter Eleven. It said:

Perhaps the most fascinating of all modern crimes is the strange case of Tito Forelli, the trapeze artist, who hurtled to his death at the gala opening of the circus in New York on September 18, 1931. To me, the enduring interest of the case lies in two facts: Firstly, that three women, all telling the same story, brought a murder conviction where there was no particle of concrete evidence; secondly, that the protagonists of the drama bore the fragrant, fairy-tale names of "White Rose" and "Red Rose." Forelli's partners in the trapeze act, the two Rosa Brothers, inevitably earned their colorful names, since one had bright red hair, while the other was prematurely white. They ...

Suddenly Iris breathed, "Peter! Listen. Someone's coming."

I STARTED. WE both stood there motionless. And, with a queer kind of menacing distinctness, footsteps sounded on the bare cement of the corridor outside. The ominous human tap-tap, coming closer and closer, made Zelide's dressing-room a trap. We had broken in unauthorized. If we were discovered there might be a scene, a scene which would make us conspicuous. And, with the police after us, that was the one thing we couldn't afford.

The footsteps were up to the door now. They stopped dead outside. I saw the curtained clothes closet. I grabbed Iris's arm. Dropping the book back on the table, I pulled her with me behind the curtain, clattering it along the iron rail to conceal us.

We were only just in time. As we pressed back against Madame Zelide's downy feather capes, I heard the door of the dressing-room open. Through a little crack in the curtains, I could see the table with the book lying on its crumpled wrapping paper. Then the person who had come into the room walked into my range of vision.

I caught my breath. He was the man from the St. Anton; the man with the gray trench coat; the man who had shot at Iris; the gunman who bit his nails!

Just seeing him was a shock. But there was something else. He was hatless, and for the first time I saw his hair. It was red.

For an excruciatingly prolonged moment he stood there by the table, gnawing at his nail. Then he picked up the Beard's book and opened it.

I saw his fingers turning the leaves rapidly. Then he gave a sharp little grunt. Furtively he slipped the book under his arm. Then, as quickly as he had come, he left.

Iris and I scrambled out of the closet together. Iris said hoarsely, "Peter, did you see his hair? The man who killed Lina and Eulalia had pure white hair, didn't he? You told me. White hair—red hair. *They* are the roses. The two gunmen were the Roses all along. And the roses they threw—they were a sort of trade-mark."

It had been as simple as that! "The protagonists bore *the fragrant, fairy-tale names of White Rose and Red Rose.*" The two trapeze artists who had murdered their partner, Tito Forelli, ten years ago, had been convicted on the evidence of three women *"all telling the same story."* The two Rosa Brothers now seemed to be taking a terrible revenge on the women whose evidence had convicted them—Eulalia, Lina, Zelide.

I remembered the Beard's sinister remark: *"The white rose and the red rose are out."* Not out in the garden. No. Out of *prison!*

Iris and I stared at each other. She said, "The Red Rose came here to steal the book because he didn't want Zelide warned. That means Zelide is still alive. That means they're still after her."

HER REASONING WAS a little higgledy-piggledy, but she'd most likely got the right idea. Emmanuel Catt must have read of the release of the two Rosa Brothers. He must have realized the great danger for the three women which that release would precipitate and he had sent each of them a copy of his book, to warn them. His warning had failed miserably with Eulalia and Lina. And now the book for Zelide had been stolen.

Zelide might be here any minute. Heaven alone knew where the drunken Beard could be found. Iris and I were the only ones now who could warn her of the terrifying vendetta which had singled her out for its third victim. Zelide's life was in our hands now.

We hurried out of the dressing-room into the corridor with no conscious plan. From far away I could hear the brassy blare of the circus band.

The passage was empty. The Red Rose had betaken himself off as neatly as he had come.

We stood there a moment ineffectually. The band had thumped into *Yankee Doodle*. Somehow that rollicking music in the distance made the immediate silence far deeper.

Suddenly the silence and the loneliness were shattered. From around the far end of the corridor debouched a wild, riotous assembly. In that motley swarm of people I made out the fat woman, the tallest man in the world, a couple of flaxen-haired midgets, youths in green tumbler uniforms, a plump, important ringmaster and a bevy of young, blond aerialists in feather capes. They were all in a state of high jubilation. Some were brandishing wine bottles, others were humming snatches of the *Mendelssohn Wedding March*. A fringe of clowns pranced around the edges like excited poodles.

There were two people in the center of the group around whom the gala pandemonium was focused. One of them was a swarthy, Greek-looking man, broad and beaming. The other was a woman whose arm was looped through his—a blonde with a mauve toque perched on stiffly waved hair.

That muscular blonde, that patently just-married blonde on the arm of her happy groom, was to me the sheerest dream of delight. There was no mistaking that flashing, toothy smile which had grinned at me from so many photographs. Zelide at last!

THE PROCESSION CAME closer and closer. The voice of the top-hatted ringmaster rose importantly: "Ah, Madame Zelide, you scare us. You are not at your hotel. You do not come for the performance. No one knows where you are. Something terrible has happened to Madame, we say. And now it is this—this happy event—a bride. Madame Zelide no longer." He kissed his own plump forefinger. "From now on, Madame Annapopaulos."

"Madame Annapopaulos!" chorused the crowd in happy unison.

"Ah," said Madame Zelide Annapopaulos coyly, beaming at her groom, "but the circus she still come first. I say to Dmitri, my career she always comes first. I say to Dmitri, whatever happens, I must make the performance. So I come. I am here."

"Madame Zelide is here for the performance," chanted the blond aerialists in well-trained reverence.

I had never seen so much innocent joy. And the irony of it surged over me. Last night Zelide had been saved by Cupid. While gunmen, out for her life's blood, had prowled the elegant lobbies of the St. Anton, she had been amorously, respectably, and securely lodged in the arms of Mr. Annapopaulos.

The procession had swarmed right up to us now and was already pouring past us through the door into Zelide's dressing-room. The happy bride and groom were swept straight past us into the room, out of sight.

"Twenty minutes, Madame," said a voice inside the room. "In twenty minutes our ballet goes on. You must be quick. Quick."

They had all vanished from sight into the room now, all except two clowns who stood in the doorway.

Iris said, "Come on, Peter. We've got to warn her before she goes on for her act."

We both started forward toward the dressing-room door. The clowns were still there, standing with their motley rainbow backs toward us.

Iris prodded at one and said, "Let us by, please. We've got to see Madame Zelide."

Inside the room we could hear loud, raucous laughs and the clinking of glasses. Slowly the two clowns turned around—a blue clown and a white clown. They stood there, blocking the doorway, staring at us.

"Please let us in," said Iris again. "We have to see Madame Zelide at once."

The eyes of the white clown flickered unpleasantly. Suddenly he swung around and shut the door of the dressing-room, so that we were barricaded from the people inside. There were only the clowns, then, and us— no one else in that deserted corridor.

"Let us by—" began Iris.

And then she stopped, with a little piping gasp. Because, very slowly, the white clown lifted a cupped hand to his mouth and gnawed at his thumbnail. The hand stayed there for a split second, then it swooped down to the broad pocket of his costume. Long before we could do anything, he had whipped out a revolver. He was aiming it directly at Iris.

"One peep out of either of you," he said, "and I'll shoot the dame in the belly."

With the gun still pointed straight at Iris, the Red Rose talked to the blue clown out of the corner of his mouth: "This is the guy and the dame I told you about—the dame I thought was Eulalia last night."

The blue clown shifted sparse shoulders and stammered, "I—I th-thought s-so."

Iris was very pale. Probably I was, too. I thought of Eulalia dead and Lina dead. I looked into those bright, fanatical eyes. The Rosa Brothers had been trapeze artists. Of course, it would have been simple for them to get themselves hired, incognito, at the circus.

I knew just how far to trust that revolver.

"Get moving," said the Red Rose. He jerked his painted head. "Down the passage. Get moving."

We had to, of course. I took Iris's hand. We started down the empty passage in the direction the Red Rose indicated. The two clowns fell in behind. The Red Rose's revolver was pressed against Iris's back.

"Left, here," said the Red Rose. "Down that passage to the left."

We turned into it, Iris and I, hand in hand. It was a narrower passage with no doors in it, a lonely, gray passage.

"If we see anyone," said the Red Rose, "and if you bat an eyelid, I shoot." After a pause, explaining, he added,

"I don't know what you know or what your game is. But we got important work to do. We ain't having you or no one else butting in—see?"

WE CAME TO the end of the corridor. There was a door, a tall, steel door. Hanging from a hook on the wall was a key. White Rose took the key. He opened the door outward. Inside there were stairs going down—and blackness.

"Turn around," said the Red Rose.

We turned around. We stared straight into his clown's face, straight at the revolver.

"Back down those stairs," he said.

We moved slowly backward, down, down into darkness. The Red Rose loomed above. Was he going to shoot now?

The revolver shifted slightly in his hand. He said, "You're lucky you're still alive. Just keep thinking about that."

Then suddenly we didn't see him any more. There was nothing but utter darkness and the vague, musty smells of a cellar. The door above us had been slammed shut. I heard the rattle of a key in the lock. Then there was no noise but our own breathing, quick, relieved. Because, as the Red Rose had said, we were alive.

We stood there, precariously, halfway down the dark stairs that led to—what?

Iris said huskily, "We must find the lights."

Lights—in that darkness!

She started up the stairs again, gropingly. I felt in my pocket for matches. I brought out a box and made a little flickering light.

"The switch must be by the door."

We reached the steel, impregnable door. There was a switch right by it. Before the match sputtered out, I twisted the switch.

Nothing happened.

I flicked it around and around. No light came. It was broken.

Iris said, "We must go down into the cellar. Maybe there's another way out."

We started down the stairs, lighting match after match, penuriously, because there weren't very many. We were down in the bowels of the cellar, tripping over old gym horses, slats, broken poles, all the odd, useless junk that ends up in a sports stadium cellar.

Then suddenly, after a match had burnt out, Iris gave a little cry, stumbled, and clutched me. "Peter, light a match. Quick. I think there are steps here."

I lit the last match but one. As its cone of flame sprouted, I saw that Iris was right. We were in a corner by the wall, and concrete stairs led up. We scrambled up them. The match went out. Falteringly I lit the last match. I held it above us. The steps seemed to lead straight to the ceiling.

"They must lead somewhere."

Iris was scrambling ahead. She reached the top. "Keep the match alight," she said; and, instantaneously, the match flickered out. There were queer, shuffling sounds in the darkness. Then Iris said, "The ceiling's wood. I think it's loose."

She gave a cry of jubilation. Because suddenly there was light—a square of light. And I saw Iris against it in silhouette. Iris, glamorous, chic, elegant, and disheveled, standing at the top of the steps, her hands above her head supporting a square trap door. There was straw everywhere.

She wriggled herself up. I went after her, squeezing through.

STRAW WAS ALL around us on the floor. Vaguely I began to realize we were in a stall, an animal stall. With a tingle of excitement I recognized it. It was empty now. But we had been here before. This was where Edwina and her train had been.

"Quick," I said, gripping Iris's arm. "We've got to get to Zelide's dressing-room. What's the time?"

Iris glanced at her little wrist watch. "Two forty-five. Maybe it's too late. Maybe she's already in the arena."

Together, we ran out of the open stall, through the great archway and headlong into the entrance to the arena itself. The music was playing, loudly, throbbingly. People were everywhere, stagehands, hangers-on, whatever they were, all crowded around the entrance to the ring.

We pushed into the crowd. Iris was ahead. Then she swung round, clutching my hand. "Look, Peter."

In front of us, almost near enough to touch and yet infinitely unget-at-able, I saw a serried row of hippy, feathered blondes marching smartly away over the red, white, and blue sawdust toward the distant center of the ring. Marching grandiosely at their head, was a single, even more majestically feathered blonde.

Madame Zelide herself!

We were at the very brink of the ring. We started running forward.

Iris called, "Madame Zelide!"

Then she stopped, because someone had gripped her from behind. I was gripped, too.

A voice said, "Are you nuts? You can't go on there. The performance is on."

We swung around desperately and stared at a lot of nondescript men.

"We've got to get to Zelide," I said. "It's a matter of life or death."

ONE OF THE men spat. Another man, an old, gnarled man with spectacles, had a newspaper. He was staring at us through the spectacles with a queer, intent sort of stare. He looked down at the front page. "Murder of Eulalia Crawford," he read. "Wanted by the police, a man and a woman answering ..."

The other men were crowding around excitedly, looking at the paper, too. We stood there, circled by them. For a moment I felt like a trapped animal.

Really before either of us knew it, Iris and I were pushing through the circle, scrambling away and running—running like mad.

"The audience," Iris panted. "We've got our tickets, Peter. That's the best place to lose ourselves—in the audience."

Vaguely I was conscious of confusion, shouts behind us, but we rushed on through the deserted side shows, past the bored caged animals, upstairs to the actual entrance to the auditorium. I had the tickets ready in my hand. We swung through doors and automatically became anonymous, just two molecules in a vast body of people.

Our seats were ringside seats, I knew—a box. No attendants were around at the moment. Iris and I started down through the tiers toward the front of the great oval house.

In the arena, the feathered, bespangled blondes were splaying out to the rhythm of the band, each of them moving to her own individual hanging trapeze. I could see the stately figure of Madame Zelide herself, bowing in the center of the ring.

We were down at the front row now. Ahead of us I could see two empty boxes. I didn't know whether one was ours or not. I didn't care. I navigated Iris ahead into one. I followed.

The sound of footsteps and voices came from behind us. Guiltily we spun around. Iris gave a little gasp. I stared—like a fool.

Because, coming down the steps between the packed rows of seats, were a man and four impeccably *Social Register* dowagers. And the man, infinitely respectable in discreet, ambassadorial serge, wore a beard—a black beard, a magnificent, godlike beard. His eyes, perhaps, were ever so slightly rheumy and morning-afterish, but he proceeded down the steps with all the sober dignity in the world.

Emmanuel Catt, America's Most Distinguished Criminologist, had come to the circus. For one paralyzed second, Iris and I stared at him. Then, as one, we pounced.

Iris said, "You! At last we've found you."

The Beard drew himself up. He fixed us both with a cold eye and said, "I haven't the pleasure of knowing you, and there is straw in your hair. Please let me pass."

So he didn't know us! So the Beard, sober among his dowagers, was a respectable Dr. Jekyll who disowned the evil, alcoholic, midnight acquaintances of his drunken Mr. Hyde other self.

"But you must remember us." Iris stared at him. "How could you forget—after last night? Pussy!"

The dowagers gave one glacial, co-operative sniff and swept into the next box. A faint flush tinged the Beard's cheeks. "Ah—last night, I—ah—was not quite myself."

"But the Rosa Brothers," said Iris wildly. "They've murdered Eulalia and Lina! It was in all the papers! And now it's Zelide."

"I haven't seen a paper," the Beard said mechanically. Then he realized what Iris had said. "Murdered Eulalia and Lina?" he gasped.

"Yes, yes. And now they're here at the circus disguised as clowns. They're after Zelide. She's right here—out in the ring."

The Beard was utterly shaken. "But she must be mad. I warned her."

SUDDENLY THERE CAME the ominous rolling of drum taps. As one, Iris and I and the astounded Beard swung around to face the ring.

The moment for the great Bird Ballet had come. Like clockwork, with the first roll on the drums, the blond "birds" lifted their arms and gripped their trapezes. Rather ponderously, they began to swing onto the trapezes and then levitate as the ropes carried them upward. The drums rolled on.

And Zelide still stood there in the center of the ring. A huge trapeze was lowering above her head. The blond "birds," in mass ascension, soared higher and higher. Vaguely I saw men up there, men in fancy costumes, hanging high up on the ropes, maneuvering them. Zelide gave a final bow.

The trapeze, lowered from above, came closer and closer. She lifted a hand for it.

And then, as the thunderous drum-roll reached its climax, something incalculably unexpected happened. Suddenly, as if materialized from nowhere, there were roses—a shower of roses tumbling down, down, splashing to the sawdust around Zelide's feet.

Red roses ... and white roses ... red roses ... and white roses ...

The audience buzzed its approval. A pretty gesture, the final touch of showmanship. But, to us, the appalling, sinister implication of those roses was almost more than we could endure.

And, as we stood there, taut as steel, helpless, Zelide reached for the trapeze. She was easing herself up onto the bar.

It was then that Iris screamed, "Look! 'Way up there in the ropes!"

She stared up. I stared up. The Beard stared up. And we saw them—saw them up there almost at the peak of the giant arched roof. Two clowns, swinging expertly on ropes, close to the cables that supported Madame Zelide's trapeze. Two clowns—a blue clown and a white clown. Clowns who, to the vast audience, were just another prop in the pageant; just part of the act.

The Red Rose and the White Rose.

And, as we stared up, I caught the sudden flash of something in the shaft of light from a baby spot. Something in the hand of the Red Rose—something gleaming and steely.

A knife!

Of course! That was the crazy plan—to cut halfway through one of Madame Zelide's trapeze ropes, to wait until she started to swing, and let her hurtle herself to her doom.

"Look!" I clutched at the Beard's arm. "The two clowns up there—they're the Roses."

"*They* dropped the roses," said Iris.

"And the Red Rose has a knife. I saw it gleaming. He was cutting through one of the trapeze ropes. Don't you see? When Zelide gets high enough, when she starts to swing ..."

For one teetering second the three of us—Iris, the Beard, and I—stood petrified in the box. Then the two clowns started swarming down their ropes. All the other men were swarming down, too—past the ascending blond aerialists. No one else but us would have singled out the Roses. No one but Iris and I, who were supposed to be safely locked in the cellar, could possibly have guessed what they had done—guessed that, right there in front of an audience of thousands, they had prepared their fantastically brazen and cunning plot to murder Zelide.

The Roses were halfway to earth. Madame Zelide was rocking on the trapeze, ready to make her triumphant aerial ascent.

OVERCOME WITH A common, desperate urgency, the Beard and Iris and I started scrambling over the front of the box and dropping down into the ring. Somewhere behind us the Beard's dowagers screamed. It was a fuse setting off a splutter of shouts and calls behind us. But, indifferent to them, we started running over the bright red, white, and blue sawdust toward Madame Zelide and the trapeze.

The drum-roll went on. Slowly, portentously, Madame Zelide and her trapeze started to rise upward, slowly upward. Attendants were running after us now, agitated, angry, with thumping footsteps and hoarse, high voices.

The Beard was ahead, his role of respectable escort to dowagers abandoned. A bearded Jupiter running with the fleetness of Mercury. We stumbled on through the sawdust. The Roses on their ropes were slipping nearer and nearer to earth. They were of vital importance. But first there was Zelide. Zelide had to be stopped in her regal ascent.

We reached the trapeze. The Beard was still ahead. It was a mad, March-hare moment. Zelide was dangling above our heads, getting higher and higher. I saw her tight-sheathed legs swinging. I saw the Beard running ahead of me, immensely dignified and portentous.

Suddenly the legs and the beard made contact. I saw Emmanuel Catt, America's Most Distinguished Criminologist, leap with extraordinary dexterity into the air. I saw his large hands fold over Zelide's ankles and tug her from the ascending trapeze.

Then, in a wild, farcical heap, the bearded dignitary and the world-famous, world-beloved aerialist were tumbling together on the sawdust in an inextricable confusion of blond hair, black beard, and roses—red and white roses.

The ringmaster was shouting and swishing with his whip. The attendants were closing in all around us. The whole vast auditorium was in an uproar. The hopeless chaos that was Emmanuel Catt and Madame Zelide squirmed in the bizarre bed of roses. But I didn't care. I felt nothing but triumph. Impossibly comic as the climax had become, we had won. Against all odds, we had saved Zelide.

The whole picture had become a kind of idiot's blur to me. Only one thing was vivid—the realization that the blue clown and the white clown had clambered down their ropes to earth. The two of them stood there for a second, staring at our swirling little group. Then they started running, swiftly for the far exit from the arena.

Vaguely I heard Madame Zelide's voice, high, shrill with furious indignation. Vaguely I heard the Beard's voice, answering gravely. But this was no time for explanations. I rushed to the Beard. I grabbed his arm.

"The White Rose and the Red Rose—they're escaping." I pointed. "There! We've got to get them."

I had a brief glimpse of Zelide's face, saw it grow pale with horror beneath the saw-dust-sprinkled blond hair. "The White Rose and the Red Rose!" she gasped. "They're *here?*"

That was all, because the Beard and Iris and I were on the run again. The three of us, buoyed up by the wild exhilaration of the chase, started dashing across the huge arena after the fast-vanishing figures of the two clowns.

THAT WAS THE maddest race in history. Behind us, stumbling, shouting, panting, came tumblers, attendants, aerialists, everyone and anyone who happened to be around. At first, I think, they were chasing us. Then, with a majestic spurt of speed, Madame Zelide, herself, caught up with us. Her tights were twisted, her blond hair was wild, but she was splendid and formidable, and she was shouting, "Get them! Murderers!"

The gigantic audience had gone crazy. I didn't blame them. They had come to see a circus. Now they had a lunatic track-race on their hands. The roar of them surged over us like a titanic wave.

"The Roses," panted Zelide. "So they try to kill me like they kill poor Forelli. They ..."

"I warned you," put in Emmanuel Catt, lumbering at her side. "I sent you a copy of my book with a note. I marked page eighty-four. I never dreamed that you ..."

"Nothing I get, no book, no note."

"The Red Rose stole it," put in Iris.

"I should have guessed they were here," panted Zelide, her blond hair streaming. "Just as I go on, Edwina, she break the line in her act; she charge at two clowns. I should have guessed."

AHEAD, WE COULD see the White Rose and the Red Rose. They had almost reached the exit. People were lounging around it, staring blankly. We shouted out to them to stop the clowns. But they didn't get the idea at all. The two Roses slipped into the little group of watchers—and disappeared.

"After them!"

We padded on at the head of our motley band. We reached the exit to the accompaniment of a final roar from the circus audience. We plunged into the little tangled group that was clustered there. I saw a large, swarthy, prosperous man in a cutaway with a pink carnation. Zelide's husband — Mr. Annapopaulos himself!

He pushed to his wife's side. "Zelide, what have we? What then goes on?"

"The Roses," stammered Zelide. "They are out of prison. They try to take their revenge, to murder me."

Everyone seethed some more.

"The clowns!" I exclaimed. "The two clowns who just ran in here. They're the murderers. They ..."

I stopped because another voice broke in harshly: "That's the guy. That guy and that lady — them's the one's wanted in the papers for the Crawford murder."

I spun round, to see the gnarled old man with the spectacles, who had almost captured Iris and me before we got to Zelide. He was pointing at us. And suddenly, from nowhere, three policemen appeared.

I never thought I'd be glad to see policemen. We rushed to them and all started talking at once. Emmanuel Catt won. The beard gave him added weight in official eyes. Maybe they even knew him by reputation.

"... tried to cut through Madame Zelide's trapeze rope and kill her ... attempted murder ... two other murders ... desperate criminals ... disguised as clowns ... just went through here ..."

Everyone started chattering then. The gnarled old murder-catcher, in particular. He pointed down a corridor and shouted, "They went that way. Two clowns."

They started running then, the three of them, down the corridor which the old man had indicated. The Beard and Iris and Madame Zelide and Mr. Annapopaulos and I followed, with the others scrambling after us.

"At least one of them has a revolver," shouted Iris. "They're dangerous."

We sped on, tumbling down one corridor, then another. There was always someone who had seen them, someone pointing ahead and shouting, "That way ... that way ..."

We passed Zelide's dressing-room. And on. Suddenly, as the corridor wound to the left, I realized what was happening. Obviously, the Roses had not planned this escape beforehand. If their cunning project had worked, they would merely have slipped down their ropes, mixed with the throng of other clowns, and actually watched the murder "accident" take place. Iris and I, by our escape from the cellar, had thrown a monkey wrench into their schedule. From now on they would have to improvise. But, circus performers from 'way back, they certainly knew all the ropes at the stadium, and they had the key to the cellar into which they had locked us. Almost definitely they would try to escape that way. Down into the cellar, locking the steel door behind them, under the ring, and then up into the animal stalls, far away from the hue and cry.

I pushed through the crowd until I could grab one of the policemen. "Let the others go on," I said. "You come with me. I think I know how we can head them off."

The policeman looked blank but came. In a second we were hurrying back against the crowd, shoving our way forcibly. Iris noticed us first, then Zelide and Mr. Annapopaulos, then the Beard. They too started pushing their way after us.

Soon the crowd, hot on the chase, had swirled on toward the cellar door, abandoning us.

"Quick," I exclaimed. "Get to the animal stalls."

They obeyed me—just because they were too dazed to do anything else. We ran on, down corridor after corridor until we reached the side entrance to the arena. We passed it, hurried under the tall archway, and then—suddenly—we were in the animal stalls. No one was there. No one at all.

Right in front of us, ranged along the walls on either side, were the elephant stalls. And the elephants themselves, their act over, lumbered around in them.

I said: "There's a trap door from the cellar. It comes up in one of the elephant stalls. I'm almost sure they'll be sneaking up that way."

"Which stall?" said the policeman sharply.

I didn't know. I looked at Iris. She was uncertain, too.

"I—I think it was over there." She pointed to a stall to the right.

We hurried toward it, a taut, keyed-up group—the Beard and the policeman, Mr. Annapopaulos with his prosperous arm around his bride's waist, Iris in the Dietrich veil, and me in what was left of my Palm Beach suit.

The elephants shuffled and watched us.

"Yes," Iris said. "I'm almost sure it's here."

She stopped, with a little scream. We all stood petrified in our steps. Because, from behind us, an all too familiar voice had sounded, steely, very, very low:

"Hands up. Every one of you. Turn around. Stick your hands up."

SLOWLY, IN UNISON, like some weird sort of circus act, the six of us wheeled around, our hands groping up into the air above our heads. We stood there, staring ... the six of us: the policeman, the criminologist, the bridegroom, the aerialist, and Iris and me, the two suckers.

Standing there in front of the other row of elephants and squarely behind two pointed revolvers, were the clowns, the white clown and the blue clown—those nightmare clowns who, once again, had turned the tables.

And it was all so tragically simple. Iris had picked the wrong stall. The Rosa Brothers had come up from the trap door behind us. They had us beautifully under control— but beautifully. Even the policeman was without a plan.

And the Roses were very much on the job. In the grotesquely painted faces the two pairs of eyes were cruelly bright and steady. The Red Rose's pink tongue slid out over his scarlet lips. He was staring straight at Zelide. He said, "Step forward, Zelide. Out here—away from the others."

Zelide gave a little moan. Mr. Annapopaulos kept his large arm stubbornly around her waist. Neither of them moved.

"We got you at last, Zelide. Just like we got Eulalia and Lina. Ten years we had to wait—ten years sweltering behind bars where you put us. You ..." The eyes were fanatical now, half crazy. "Get forward."

The elephants weaved with their trunks all around us, shuffled their straw, flicked their ears, and looked bored. Somewhere along the line one of them trumpeted and started an uproarious clatter.

Zelide looked grimly at Mr. Annapopaulos. "It is no use, Dmitri. You too must not suffer. I go."

"No, no ..."

"Yes."

I admired her then. Zelide was a really brave woman.

"Come out, Zelide." The White Rose had the rest of us covered. The Red Rose kept his revolver pointed on Zelide. She took a step forward—very erect.

"This way." The Red Rose jerked along the stalls with his revolver. "Down here."

Zelide moved forward. The Red Rose stepped in behind her. They started up the aisle between the elephant stalls. It was horrible. A sort of mock execution, a terrible, half-mad mockery of an execution.

Zelide moved along. The elephant down the line trumpeted again. Zelide walked more quickly. She reached a stall. The Red Rose was close behind her. Then, like lightning, Zelide dived into the open stall. There was a scuffling and the wild trumpeting again. Then Zelide's voice screaming, "Edwina! Get him, Edwina! The Red Rose! Get him!"

It was sheer lunacy from then on. The Red Rose stiffened. I saw him jerk the revolver around. I saw his finger on the trigger. A shot was fired. The trumpeting teetered over into a wild, animal scream of fury. Then an elephant was charging—a vast mammoth of an elephant charging, breaking out of the stall, head raised, trunk bristling, a huge, inexorable elephant with an immense pink ribbon around its neck. Edwina!

I SAW THE Red Rose hesitate, stare in horror at that terrifying sight. Then he started to run, and Edwina was lumbering after him.

"Get him, Edwina. Get him!"

The White Rose still had us covered. At least, up till then, he had. But, as Zelide's voice rang out again, he faltered and glanced over his shoulder. Instantly, all with the same idea, Mr. Annapopaulos, the policeman, the Beard, and I, leaped forward, knocked the revolver out of his hand, and tumbled him to the floor.

I scrambled up, leaving the White Rose to the tender mercies of the others. I wheeled around to Edwina. I was just in time to see her head trundle down. Then there was a scream—a human scream. I saw the immense pink ribbon flapping. Then I saw other colors. I saw the white of the clown, waving helplessly in the air, encircled by the viselike trunk.

Zelide ran out of the stall. Iris and I ran forward, too.

For a moment the Red Rose was, madly, up in the air there, screaming. Then he was hurled to the ground.

Zelide rushed forward. "Edwina!" she shouted. "Leave him alone now. Don't kill him. Leave him, Edwina!"

Even in its fury, the elephant seemed to hear and obey. She backed, trumpeting, shaking her trunk. Zelide and Iris and I rushed forward. The Red Rose was there, twisting and turning in the straw. I pounced on him. He had no strength left. I saw Zelide's eyes gleaming with triumph.

"Edwina—she save me. I know if I can get him to her stall, she save me. The Roses—they remember and hate for ten years. But Edwina remembers forever. Edwina, the elephant, she never forgets."

The others were hurrying to us now, lugging the White Rose with them. I pulled the dazed Red Rose to his feet. We all crowded around.

"Edwina, she is shot. But a little revolver shot—to Edwina it is a mere flea-bite, yes?" Zelide was coping enthusiastically with Edwina. And Edwina seemed to love it. She was puffing a little, but she was perfectly calm again. And her trunk stopped weaving. Ever so delicately, she curled its tip around Zelide's wrist.

"Edwina!" we shouted. "Edwina! ... Bravo, Edwina!"

And she smirked. I swear she did....

THERE WAS HIGH festivity and merry-making in the dressing-room of Madame Zelide, world-famous, world-beloved aerialist. The Red Rose and the White Rose had been taken away by the policemen. Soon we, too, would have to follow to the police station. But at the moment joy was unconfined.

Sweet red wine was pouring with abandon. Madame Zelide and Mr. Annapopaulos, giving vent to their warm Southern temperaments, were kissing everyone at random. They kissed me, both of them; they kissed Iris. They even dared to kiss the Beard, who, dowagers forgotten, was beaming broadly, perched on a stool. Everything was confusion.

No one seemed to realize that Iris and I were still at sea. We'd been through hell-fire; we'd run the gamut of every kind of emotion; we'd got straw in our hair—actually and figuratively. But we still had only the mistiest idea of what it was all about.

That didn't seem to matter.

AND, AT THE peak of the toasts, the door burst open, and the ringmaster, resplendent in top hat and tails, surged in on a wave of enthusiastic blond aerialists. He rushed to Madame Zelide and kissed her. Then he swept the Beard and Iris and me into a mass embrace.

"You save the circus!" he said. "When it happens, when you tug Madame from the trapeze, I say—the end. The most terrible thing! But now we find the trapeze rope—she was half cut through. Those fiends, those madmen! Certainly Madame would have plunged to her death. You save us from the most terrible of tragedies." His enthusiasm mounted: "Free tickets. For every performance I give you free tickets. The best—boxes."

I managed to disentangle myself. "But if only someone would tell us something, anything. For example: Why did Edwina hate the Roses?"

Madame Zelide gulped red wine and stared. "But they were so cruel to her—always. Edwina, she love Tito Forelli. The Roses hate him. Once they attack him, the two of them together, and Edwina went to his rescue. After that they hate her, too. Always they think out mean, cruel tricks to plague her. Edwina does not forget. No."

"But why," added Iris, in an attempt to get someone to stick to the point, "why did the Roses hate Tito Forelli?"

Emmanuel Catt rose majestically. We were obviously now entering his domain. "That," he began, "is one of the most fascinating cases in criminal history. I have—ah—made a study of it in my book, *Crimes of Our Times*. I shall give you a copy. The murder of Tito Forelli shows the psychopathic jealousy motive coupled with the perfect crime and the relentless Nemesis as supremely as any ..."

"But it is so easy to say," broke in Zelide, who seemed in no mood to hand over the spotlight to a mere criminologist. "Ten years ago Forelli is the partner of the Roses in a trapeze act. He is the star, by far the best. And the Roses were madly jealous."

"Professional jealousy at its ..." began the Beard.

"And there was Eulalia Crawford, too," Zelide dived in. "The girl who then makes the carnival figures for us. She is beautiful, attractive. And she loves Forelli. That makes the Roses even more madly jealous, because the Red Rose, too, loves Eulalia. The White Rose, he was never so bright in the head, just the—how you say?—shadow of his brother, ready to do anything for the Red Rose, die for him, kill for him."

"A typical moronic assistant, a gangster's bodyguard, a ..."

"And so, the Red Rose, his jealousy gets stronger and stronger and his hate. And, together with his brother, he thinks out a plan—a plan to kill Forelli so that the Red Rose can have Eulalia. The plan, it is perfect, they think. During the trapeze act, they will drop Forelli, they will send him hurtling to his doom. All the world will think it is an accident, yes—a simple accident. It happens often with aerialists. No one will suspect."

ZELIDE PAUSED FOR breath. The Beard charged in: "The perfect theoretical murder, no evidence, no clues ..."

"Dmitri, more wine for Mr. Catt," broke in Zelide torridly. "You see, Mr. Duluth, it worked, their plan—yes. And they were proud—proud as clever murderers who would never be discovered. In the papers, everything, it said—accident; Tito Forelli die by accident. Partners absolved. Eulalia then was to be for the Red Rose. But they were fools, stupid fools. For Eulalia hated Red Rose and suspected them. She was cunning, Eulalia. She know they are vain, boastful. She praises them, how clever they are, feeds their vanity. There is little Lina, she was with our ballet then, and she was Eulalia's greatest friend. There was I, too—I then was only an unknown little aerialist, and I, too, am a friend of Eulalia's. She comes to ask, makes us hide in a room, and she brings the Roses in. She praises them, so cunningly: '*You are so clever and so smart, so much more clever than Forelli.*' And they fall in the trap. While Lina and I are there as witnesses, we hear the Red Rose laugh and say boastfully to Eulalia, '*Sure, we more clever than that Forelli. We fixed him. We got his number okay.*'"

"So Eulalia," broke in the Beard gravely, "tricked them through their vanity into a murder confession in front of witnesses. Although there was no shred of evidence, the three women went to the police. The police believed them. And, afterward, the jury believed them, too. The Rosa Brothers were sent to prison as murderers for ten years."

"And they never forgive us," said Zelide. "Oh, in time we forget. Until this afternoon everything was from my mind. But the Roses never forgot."

So that was it! Sketchily, vaguely as it had been told in competitive duet, the story emerged plain as glass. Two mean, revengeful, small-time crooks who had planned what they thought was the perfect murder, only to be outwitted by three girls. Two small-time crooks, brooding in prison, harping on their wounded pride and their hatred for the woman one of them had loved and her friends; two crooks, distorted by their hate, living only for one thing—release and revenge, a second chance to prove themselves smarter than the women who had defeated them.

And the revenge of the Rosas had reaped terrible havoc—for themselves, for two of the women, for all of us. But it was over now, thanks to Edwina, whose slow, stubborn impulse to revenge had been even stronger than theirs.

Everyone, the ringmaster, the fluttering blond "birds," Mr. Annapopaulos, they had all been listening to that strange tale in rapt astonishment.

But the Beard was now the central figure. He stood in Jovelike splendor, twisting the glass of cheap red wine rather shudderingly. I could imagine how he felt about it after last night's champagne.

"All along," he said, "since my study of the case, I felt there would be great danger when the Rosa Brothers were released. I know their type—the little Caesars, the little men with the big egos and a vast capacity for hate and revenge. Yesterday I tried to warn the three women. I should have done much more. But last night I—was unfortunately not quite myself."

He paused there and looked at Iris. The black beard twitched. Slowly, almost infinitesimally, an eyelid lowered in a wink. It was clear that Emmanuel Catt's lamentable exuberance of the night before was to be our own particular little secret.

"I admit I was a failure, a tragic failure," he said. "But now I drink to the two people who, knowing nothing at all about the issues at stake, managed, by their ingenuity and their courage, at least to save—Madame Zelide. I propose a toast. I toast the two most resourceful people I have ever encountered. I toast Mr. and Mrs. Duluth!"

Everyone grabbed glasses, even the respectful blond aerialists. There were shouts, applause, confusion. Glasses were waved on high. Feather capes fluttered. And, in noble diapason, the room rocked to the chorus: "Mr. and Mrs. Duluth!"

I TURNED TO look at Iris. How did she manage to be so utterly beautiful after all we'd been through? I lifted my glass to her. She lifted hers to me. She smiled—that quick, dazzling smile which always catches the breath right out of me.

"Mr. and Mrs. Duluth," she breathed. "Twelve months later, darling—and it still sounds voluptuous."

I leaned forward and kissed her. Her lips were so soft and warm, so very, very right.

"Mr. and Mrs. Duluth!" shouted the blond "birds" with an abandon which almost certainly stemmed from the red wine. "Bravo, Mr. and Mrs. Duluth! Bravo!"

I hated taking my lips away from Iris's. I could have done without the ecstatic aerialists, too, and Madame Zelide, and Mr. Annapopaulos, and the ringmaster, and the Beard.

But I didn't really care. Because, suddenly, I was sure of one thing: against all odds, it had turned out to be a good wedding anniversary, after all. It certainly had.

An honest-to-goodness, supercolossal wedding anniversary!

Puzzle for Poppy

Yes, Miss Crump," snapped Iris into the phone. "No, Miss Crump. Oh, nuts, Miss Crump."

My wife flung down the receiver.

"Well?" I asked.

"She won't let us use the patio. It's that dog, that great fat St. Bernard. It mustn't be disturbed."

"Why?"

"It has to be alone with its beautiful thoughts. It's going to become a mother. Peter, it's revolting. There must be something in the lease."

"There isn't," I said.

When I'd rented our half of this La Jolla hacienda for my shore leave, the lease specified that all rights to the enclosed patio belonged to our eccentric co-tenant. It oughtn't to have mattered, but it did because Iris had recently skyrocketed to fame as a movie star and it was impossible for us to appear on the streets without being mobbed. For the last couple of days we had been virtually beleaguered in our apartment. We were crazy about being beleaguered together, but even Héloise and Abelard needed a little fresh air once in a while.

That's why the patio was so important.

Iris was staring through the locked French windows at the forbidden delights of the patio. Suddenly she turned.

"Peter, I'll die if I don't get things into my lungs — ozone and things. We'll just have to go to the beach."

"And be torn limb from limb by your public again?"

"I'm sorry, darling. I'm terribly sorry." Iris unzipped herself from her housecoat and scrambled into slacks and a shirt-waist. She tossed me my naval hat. "Come, Lieutenant — to the slaughter."

When we emerged on the street, we collided head on with a man carrying groceries into the house. As we disentangled ourselves from celery stalks, there was a click and a squeal of delight followed by a powerful whistle. I turned to see a small girl who had been lying in wait with a camera. She was an unsightly little girl with sandy pigtails and a brace on her teeth.

"Geeth," she announced. "I can get two buckth for thith thnap from Barney Thtone. He'th thappy about you, Mith Duluth."

Other children, materializing in response to her whistle, were galloping toward us. The grocery man came out of the house. Passers-by stopped, stared and closed in — a woman in scarlet slacks, two sailors, a flurry of bobby-soxers, a policeman.

"This," said Iris grimly, "is the end."

She escaped from her fans and marched back to the two front doors of our hacienda. She rang the buzzer on the door that wasn't ours. She rang persistently. At length there was the clatter of a chain sliding into place and the door opened wide enough to reveal the face of Miss Crump. It was a small, faded face with a most uncordial expression.

"Yes?" asked Miss Crump.

"We're the Duluths," said Iris. "I just called you. I know about your dog, but ..."

"Not *my* dog," corrected Miss Crump. "Mrs. Wilberframe's dog. The late Mrs. Wilberframe of Glendale who has a nephew and a niece-in-law of whom I know a great deal in Ogden Bluffs, Utah. At least, they *ought* to be in Ogden Bluffs."

This unnecessary information was flung at us like a challenge. Then Miss Crump's face flushed into sudden, dimpled pleasure.

"Duluth! Iris Duluth. You're *the* Iris Duluth of the movies?"

"Yes," said Iris.

"Oh, why didn't you tell me over the phone? My favorite actress! How exciting! Poor thing — mobbed by your fans. Of course you may use the patio. I will give you the key to open your French windows. Any time."

Miraculously the chain was off the door. It opened halfway and then stopped. Miss Crump was staring at me with a return of suspicion.

"You *are* Miss Duluth's husband?"

"Mrs. Duluth's husband," I corrected her. "Lieutenant Duluth."

She still peered. "I mean, you have proof?"

I was beyond being surprised by Miss Crump. I fumbled from my wallet a dog-eared snapshot of Iris and me in full wedding regalia outside the church. Miss Crump studied it carefully and then returned it.

"You must please excuse me. What a sweet bride! It's just that I can't be too careful — for Poppy."

"Poppy?" queried Iris. "The St. Bernard?"

Miss Crump nodded. "It is Poppy's house, you see. Poppy pays the rent."

"The dog," said Iris faintly, "pays the rent?"

"Yes, my dear. Poppy is very well-to-do. She is hardly more than a puppy, but she is one of the richest dogs, I suppose, in the whole world."

Although we entertained grave doubts as to Miss Crump's sanity, we were soon in swimming suits and stepping through our open French windows into the sunshine of the patio. Miss Crump introduced us to Poppy.

In spite of our former prejudices, Poppy disarmed us immediately. She was just a big, bouncing, natural girl unspoiled by wealth. She greeted us with great thumps of her tail. She leaped up at Iris, dabbing at her cheek with a long, pink tongue. Later, when we had settled on striped mattresses under orange trees, she curled into a big clumsy ball at my side and laid her vast muzzle on my stomach.

"Look, she likes you." Miss Crump was glowing. "Oh, I knew she would!"

Iris, luxuriating in the sunshine, asked the polite question. "Tell us about Poppy. How did she make her money?"

"Oh, she did not make it. She inherited it." Miss Crump sat down on a white iron chair. "Mrs. Wilberframe was a very wealthy woman. She was devoted to Poppy."

"And left her all her money?" I asked.

"Not quite all. There was a little nest egg for me. I was her companion, you see, for many years. But I am to look after Poppy. That is why I received the nest egg. Poppy pays me a generous salary too." She fingered nondescript beads at her throat. "Mrs. Wilberframe was anxious for Poppy to have only the best and I am sure I try to do the right thing. Poppy has the master bedroom, of course. I take the little one in front. And then, if Poppy has steak for dinner, I have hamburger." She stared intensely. "I would not have an easy moment if I felt that Poppy did not get the best."

Poppy, her head on my stomach, coughed. She banged her tail against the flagstones apologetically.

Iris reached across me to pat her. "Has she been rich for long?"

"Oh, no, Mrs. Wilberframe passed on only a few weeks ago." Miss Crump paused. "And it has been a great responsibility for me." She paused again and then blurted: "You're my friends, aren't you? Oh, I am sure you are. Please, please, won't you help me? I am all alone and I am so frightened."

"Frightened?" I looked up and, sure enough, her little bird face was peaked with fear.

"For Poppy." Miss Crump leaned forward. "Oh, Lieutenant, it is like a nightmare. Because I know. I just know they are trying to murder her!"

"They?" Iris sat up straight.

"Mrs. Wilberframe's nephew and his wife. From Ogden Bluffs, Utah."

"You mentioned them when you opened the door."

"I mention them to everyone who comes to the house. You see, I do not know what they look like and I do not want them to think I am not on my guard."

I watched her. She might have looked like a silly spinster with a bee in her bonnet. She didn't. She looked nice and quite sane, only scared.

"Oh, they are not good people. Not at all. There is nothing they would not stoop to. Back in Glendale, I found pieces of meat in the front yard. Poisoned meat, I know. And on a lonely road, they shot at Poppy. Oh, the police laughed at me. A car backfiring, they said. But I know differently. I know they won't stop till Poppy is dead." She threw her little hands up to her face. "I ran away from them in Glendale. That is why I came to La Jolla. But they have caught up with us. I know. Oh, dear, poor Poppy who is so sweet without a nasty thought in her head."

Poppy, hearing her name mentioned, smiled and panted.

"But this nephew and his wife from Ogden Bluffs, why should they want to murder her?" My wife's eyes were gleaming with a detective enthusiasm I knew of old. "Are they after her money?"

"Of course," said Miss Crump passionately. "It's the will. The nephew is Mrs. Wilberframe's only living relative, but she deliberately cut him off and I am sure I do not blame her. All the money goes to Poppy and — er — Poppy's little ones."

"Isn't the nephew contesting a screwy will like that?" I asked.

"Not yet. To contest a will takes a great deal of money — lawyers fees and things. It would be much, much cheaper for him to kill Poppy. You see, one thing is not covered by the will. If Poppy were to die before she became a mother, the nephew would inherit the whole estate. Oh, I have done everything in my power. The moment the — er — suitable season arrived, I found a husband for Poppy. In a few weeks now, the — the little ones are expected. But these next few weeks ..."

Miss Crump dabbed at her eyes with a small handkerchief. "Oh, the Glendale police were most unsympathetic. They even mentioned the fact that the sentence for shooting or killing a dog in this state is shockingly light — a small fine at most. I called the police here and asked for protection. They said they'd send a man around some time but they were hardly civil. So you see, there is no protection from the law and no redress. There is no one to help me."

"You've got us," said Iris in a burst of sympathy.

"Oh ... oh ..." The handkerchief fluttered from Miss Crump's face. "I knew you were my friends. You dear, dear things. Oh, Poppy, they are going to help us."

Poppy, busy licking my stomach, did not reply. Somewhat appalled by Iris' hasty promise but ready to stand by her, I said:

"Sure, we'll help, Miss Crump. First, what's the nephew's name?"

"Henry. Henry Blodgett. But he won't use that name. Oh, no, he will be too clever for that."

"And you don't know what he looks like?"

"Mrs. Wilberframe destroyed his photograph many years ago when he bit her as a small boy. With yellow curls, I understand. That is when the trouble between them started."

"At least you know what age he is?"

"He should be about thirty."

"And the wife?" asked Iris.

"I know nothing about her," said Miss Crump coldly, "except that she is supposed to be a red-headed person, a former actress."

"And what makes you so sure one or both of them have come to La Jolla?"

Miss Crump folded her arms in her lap. "Last night. A telephone call."

"A telephone call?"

"A voice asking if I was Miss Crump, and then — silence." Miss Crump leaned toward me. "Oh, now they know I am here. They know I never let Poppy out. They know every morning I search the patio for meat, traps. They must realize that the only possible way to reach her is to enter the house."

"Break in?"

Miss Crump shook her tight curls. "It is possible. But I believe they will rely on guile rather than violence. It is against that we must be on our guard. You are the only people who have come to the door since that telephone call. Now anyone else that comes to your apartment or mine, whatever their excuse ..." She lowered her voice. "Anyone may be Henry Blodgett or his wife and we will have to outwit them."

A fly settled on one of Poppy's valuable ears. She did not seem to notice it. Miss Crump watched us earnestly and then gave a self-scolding cluck.

"Dear me, here I have been burdening you with Poppy's problems and you must be hungry. How about a little salad for luncheon? I always feel guilty about eating in the middle of the day when Poppy has her one meal at night. But with guests — yes, and allies — I am sure Mrs. Wilberframe would not have grudged the expense."

With a smile that was half-shy, half-conspiratorial, she fluttered away.

I looked at Iris. "Well," I said, "is she a nut or do we believe her?"

"I rather think," said my wife, "that we believe her."

"Why?"

"Just because." Iris' face wore the entranced expression which had won her so many fans in her last picture. "Oh, Peter, don't you see what fun it will be? A beautiful St. Bernard in peril. A wicked villain with golden curls who bit his aunt."

"He won't have golden curls any more," I said. "He's a big boy now."

Iris, her body warm from the sun, leaned over me and put both arms around Poppy's massive neck.

"Poor Poppy," she said. "Really, this shouldn't happen to a dog!"

THE FIRST THING happened some hours after Miss Crump's little salad luncheon while Iris and I were still sunning ourselves. Miss Crump, who had been preparing Poppy's dinner and her own in her apartment, came running to announce:

"There is a man at the door! He claims he is from the electric light company to read the meter. Oh, dear, if he is legitimate and we do not let him in, there will be trouble with the electric light company and if ..." She wrung her hands. "Oh, what shall we do?"

I reached for a bathrobe. "You and Iris stay here. And for Mrs. Wilberframe's sake, hang on to Poppy."

I found the man outside the locked front door. He was about thirty with thinning hair and wore an army discharge button. He showed me his credentials. They seemed in perfect order. There was nothing for it but to let him in. I took him into the kitchen where Poppy's luscious steak and Miss Crump's modest hamburger were lying where Miss Crump had left them on the table. I hovered over the man while he located the meter. I never let him out of my sight until he had departed. In answer to Miss Crump's anxious questioning, I could only say that if the man had been Henry Blodgett he knew how much electricity she'd used in the past month—but that was all.

The next caller showed up a few minutes later. Leaving Iris, indignant at being out of things, to stand by Poppy, Miss Crump and I handled the visitor. This time it was a slim, brash girl with bright auburn hair and a navy-blue slack suit. She was, she said, the sister of the woman who owned the hacienda. She wanted a photograph for the newspapers — a photograph of her Uncle William who had just been promoted to Rear Admiral in the Pacific. The photograph was in a trunk in the attic.

Miss Crump, reacting to the unlikeliness of the request, refused entry. The red-head wasn't the type that wilted. When she started talking darkly of eviction, I overrode Miss Crump and offered to conduct her to the attic. The girl gave me one quick, experienced look and flounced into the hall.

The attic was reached by the back stairs through the kitchen. I conducted the red-head directly to her claimed destination. There were trunks. She searched through them. At length she produced a photograph of a limp young man in a raccoon coat.

"My Uncle William," she snapped, "as a youth."

"Pretty," I said.

I took her back to the front door. On the threshold she gave me another of her bold, appraising stares.

"You know something?" she said. "I was hoping you'd make a pass at me in the attic."

"Why?" I asked.

"So's I could tear your ears off."

She left. If she had been Mrs. Blodgett, she knew how to take care of herself, she knew how many trunks there were in the attic — and that was all.

Iris and I had dressed and were drinking Daiquiris under a green and white striped umbrella when Miss Crump appeared followed by a young policeman. She was very pleased about the policeman. He had come, she said, in answer to her complaint. She showed him Poppy; she babbled out her story of the Blodgetts. He obviously thought she was a harmless lunatic, but she didn't seem to realize it. After she had let him out, she settled beamingly down with us.

"I suppose," said Iris, "you asked him for his credentials?"

"I ..." Miss Crump's face clouded. "My dear, you don't think that perhaps he wasn't a real police ... ?"

"To me," said Iris, "everyone's a Blodgett until proved to the contrary."

"Oh, dear," said Miss Crump.

Nothing else happened. By evening Iris and I were back in our part of the house. Poppy had hated to see us go. We had hated to leave her. A mutual crush had developed between us.

But now we were alone again, the sinister Blodgetts did not seem very substantial. Iris made a creditable *Boeuf Stroganov* from yesterday's left-overs and changed into a lime green négligée which would have inflamed the whole Pacific Fleet. I was busy being a sailor on leave with his girl when the phone rang. I reached over Iris for the receiver, said "Hello," and then sat rigid listening.

It was Miss Crump's voice. But something was horribly wrong with it. It came across hoarse and gasping.

"Come," it said. "Oh, come. The French windows. Oh, please …"

The voice faded. I heard the clatter of a dropped receiver.

"It must be Poppy," I said to Iris. "Quick."

We ran out into the dark patio. Across it, I could see the light French windows to Miss Crump's apartment. They were half open, and as I looked Poppy squirmed through to the patio. She bounded toward us, whining.

"Poppy's all right," said Iris. "Quick!"

We ran to Miss Crump's windows. Poppy barged past us into the living room. We followed. All the lights were on. Poppy had galloped around a high-backed davenport. We went to it and looked over it.

Poppy was crouching on the carpet, her huge muzzle dropped on her paws. She was howling and staring straight at Miss Crump.

Poppy's paid companion was on the floor too. She lay motionless on her back, her legs twisted under her, her small, grey face distorted, her lips stretched in a dreadful smile.

I knelt down by Poppy. I picked up Miss Crump's thin wrist and felt for the pulse. Poppy was still howling. Iris stood, straight and white.

"Peter, tell me. Is she dead?"

"Not quite. But only just not quite. Poison. It looks like strychnine. …"

We called a doctor. We called the police. The doctor came, muttered a shocked diagnosis of strychnine poisoning and rushed Miss Crump to the hospital. I asked if she had a chance. He didn't answer. I knew what that meant. Soon the police came and there was so much to say and do and think that I hadn't time to brood about poor Miss Crump.

We told Inspector Green the Blodgett story. It was obvious to us that somehow Miss Crump had been poisoned by them in mistake for Poppy. Since no one had entered the house that day except the three callers, one of them, we said, must have been a Blodgett. All the Inspector had to do, we said, was to locate those three people and find out which was a Blodgett.

Inspector Green watched us poker-faced and made no comment. After he'd left, we took the companionless Poppy back to our part of the house. She climbed on the bed and stretched out between us, her tail thumping, her head flopped on the pillows. We didn't have the heart to evict her. It was not one of our better nights.

Early next morning, a policeman took us to Miss Crump's apartment. Inspector Green was waiting in the living room. I didn't like his stare.

"We've analyzed the hamburger she was eating last night," he said. "There was enough strychnine in it to kill an elephant."

"Hamburger!" exclaimed Iris. "Then that proves she was poisoned by the Blodgetts!"

"Why?" asked Inspector Green.

"They didn't know how conscientious Miss Crump was. They didn't know she always bought steak for Poppy and hamburger for herself. They saw the steak and the hamburger and they naturally assumed the hamburger was for Poppy, so they poisoned that."

"That's right," I cut in. "The steak and the hamburger were lying right on the kitchen table when all three of those people came in yesterday."

"I see," said the Inspector.

He nodded to a policeman who left the room and returned with three people — the balding young man from the electric light company, the red-headed vixen, and the young policeman. None of them looked happy.

"You're willing to swear," the Inspector asked us, "that these were the only three people who entered this house yesterday."

"Yes," said Iris.

"And you think one of them is either Blodgett or his wife?"

"They've got to be."

Inspector Green smiled faintly. "Mr. Burns here has been with the electric light company for five years except for a year when he was in the army. The electric light company is willing to vouch for that. Miss Curtis has been identified as the sister of the lady who owns this house and the niece of Rear Admiral Moss. She has no connection with any Blodgetts and has never been in Utah." He paused. "As for Officer Patterson, he has been a member of the police force here for eight years. I personally sent him around yesterday to follow up Miss Crump's complaint."

The Inspector produced an envelope from his pocket and tossed it to me. "I've had these photographs of Mr. and Mrs. Henry Blodgett flown from the files of the Ogden Bluffs *Tribune*."

I pulled the photographs out of the envelope. We stared at them. Neither Mr. or Mrs. Blodgett looked at all the sort of person you would like to know. But neither of them bore the slightest resemblance to any of the three suspects in front of us.

"It might also interest you," said the Inspector quietly, "that I've checked with the Ogden Bluffs police. Mr. Blodgett has been sick in bed for over a week and his wife has been nursing him. There is a doctor's certificate to that effect."

Inspector Green gazed down at his hands. They were competent hands. "It looks to me that the whole Blodgett story was built up in Miss Crump's mind — or yours." His grey eyes stared right through us. "If we have to eliminate the Blodgetts and these three people from suspicion, that leaves only two others who had the slightest chance of poisoning the hamburger."

Iris blinked. "Us?"

"You," said Inspector Green almost sadly.

THEY DIDN'T ARREST US, of course. We had no conceivable motive. But Inspector Green questioned us minutely and when he left there was a policeman lounging outside our door.

We spent a harried afternoon racking our brains and getting nowhere. Iris was the one who had the inspiration. Suddenly, just after she had fed Poppy the remains of the *Stroganov*, she exclaimed:

"Good heavens above, of course!"

"Of course, what?"

She spun to me, her eyes shining. "Barney Thtone," she lisped. "Why didn't we realize? Come on!"

She ran out of the house into the street. She grabbed the lounging policeman by the arm.

"You live here," she said. "Who's Barney Stone?"

"Barney Stone?" The policeman stared. "He's the son of the druggist on the corner."

Iris raced me to the drugstore. She was attracting quite a crowd. The policeman followed, too.

In the drugstore, a thin young man with spectacles stood behind the prescription counter.

"Mr. Stone?" asked Iris.

His mouth dropped open. "Gee, Miss Duluth. I never dreamed … Gee, Miss Duluth, what can I do for you? Cigarettes? An alarm clock?"

"A little girl," said Iris. "A little girl with sandy pigtails and a brace on her teeth. What's her name? Where does she live?"

Barney Stone said promptly: "You mean Daisy Kornfeld. Kind of homely. Just down the block. 712. Miss Duluth, I certainly …"

"Thanks," cut in Iris and we were off again with our ever growing escort.

Daisy was sitting in the Kornfeld parlor, glumly thumping the piano. Ushered in by an excited, cooing Mrs. Kornfeld, Iris interrupted Daisy's rendition of *The Jolly Farmer*.

"Daisy, that picture you took of me yesterday to sell to Mr. Stone, is it developed yet?"

"Geeth no, Mith Duluth. I ain't got the developing money yet. Theventy-five thenth. Ma don't give me but a nickel an hour for practithing thith gothdarn piano."

"Here." Iris thrust a ten-dollar bill into her hand. "I'll buy the whole roll. Run get the camera. We'll have it developed right away."

"Geeth." The mercenary Daisy stared with blank incredulity at the ten-dollar bill.

I stared just as blankly myself. I wasn't being bright at all.

I WASN'T MUCH brighter an hour later. We were back in our apartment, waiting for Inspector Green. Poppy, all for love, was trying to climb into my lap. Iris, who had charmed Barney Stone into developing Daisy's films, clutched the yellow envelope of snaps in her hand. She had sent our policeman away on a secret mission, but an infuriating passion for the dramatic had kept her from telling or showing me anything. I had to wait for Inspector Green.

Eventually Iris' policeman returned and whispered with her in the hall. Then Inspector Green came. He looked cold and hostile. Poppy didn't like him. She growled. Sometimes Poppy was smart.

Inspector Green said: "You've been running all over town. I told you to stay here."

"I know." Iris' voice was meek. "It's just that I wanted to solve poor Miss Crump's poisoning."

"Solve it?" Inspector Green's query was skeptical.

"Yes. It's awfully simple really. I can't imagine why we didn't think of it from the start."

"You mean you know who poisoned her?"

"Of course." Iris smiled, a maddening smile. "Henry Blodgett."

"But ..."

"Check with the airlines. I think you'll find that Blodgett flew in from Ogden Bluffs a few days ago and flew back today. As for his being sick in bed under his wife's care, I guess that'll make Mrs. Blodgett an accessory before the fact, won't it?"

Inspector Green was pop-eyed.

"Oh, it's my fault really," continued Iris. "I said no one came to the house yesterday except those three people. There was someone else, but he was so ordinary, so run-of-the-mill, that I forgot him completely."

I was beginning to see then. Inspector Green snapped: "And this run-of-the-mill character?"

"The man," said Iris sweetly, "who had the best chance of all to poison the hamburger, *the man who delivered it —* the man from the Supermarket."

"We don't have to guess. We have proof." Iris fumbled in the yellow envelope. "Yesterday morning as we were going out, we bumped into the man delivering Miss Crump's groceries. Just at that moment, a sweet little girl took a snap of us. This snap."

She selected a print and handed it to Inspector Green. I moved to look at it over his shoulder.

"I'm afraid Daisy is an impressionistic photographer," murmured Iris. "That hip on the right is me. The buttocks are my husband. But the figure in the middle — quite a masterly likeness of Henry Blodgett, isn't it? Of course, there's the grocery apron, the unshaven chin ..."

She was right. Daisy had only winged Iris and me but with the grocery man she had scored a direct hit. And the grocery man was unquestionably Henry Blodgett.

Iris nodded to her policeman. "Sergeant Blair took a copy of the snap around the neighborhood groceries. They recognized Blodgett at the Supermarket. They hired him day before yesterday. He made a few deliveries this morning, including Miss Crump's, and took a powder without his pay."

"Well ..." stammered Inspector Green. "Well ..."

"Just how many charges can you get him on?" asked my wife hopefully. "Attempted homicide, conspiracy to defraud, illegal possession of poisonous drugs.... The rat, I hope you give him the works when you get him."

"We'll get him all right," said Inspector Green.

Iris leaned over and patted Poppy's head affectionately.

"Don't worry, darling. I'm sure Miss Crump will get well and we'll throw a lovely christening party for your little strangers...."

Iris was right about the Blodgetts. Henry got the works. And his wife was held as an accessory. Iris was right about Miss Crump too. She is still in the hospital but improving steadily and will almost certainly be well enough to attend the christening party.

Meanwhile, at her request, Poppy is staying with us, awaiting maternity with rollicking unconcern.

It's nice having a dog who pays the rent.

Death and the Rising Star

W hen I first heard of Didi Cheri, I had no idea who she was and cared less. Everything was going fine with *Larksong*. Audrey Harris had read the script in London and was crazy to play Stella. She hadn't actually signed, but I was expecting the clinching cable any minute. With Audrey sewed up, I was as sure—as any poor Broadway producer can be—that Peter Duluth, Inc., had a smash hit on its hands.

Didi Cheri! What a preposterous name! That's all I thought. No one, not even a Wampus Baby Star of 1928, deserved to be called Didi Cheri.

Western Union seemed to agree with me, for at the end of the telegram from Beverly Hills they had written the name out a second time: DIDI CHERI QUERY.

The telegram itself did not mince matters.

UNDERSTAND YOU ARE CASTING LARKSONG ONLY ONE ACTRESS IN WORLD CAN DO STELLA THE ONE THE ONLY THE INCOMPA-RABLE DIDI CHERI PLAZA 9-0999 LOVE AND TO IRIS

DANNY KAYE

Iris, my wife, happened to be in the office. She'd dropped in for a moment on her way to a visit with her mother in Schenectady. I showed her the telegram.

"Didi Cheri," she said. "It sounds like the fourth row at the Folies Bergéres. But overdone. Is it one of Danny's gags?"

Five minutes after she'd left, Bill Austin, the young stage manager I'd just hired for *Larksong*, buzzed me from the next office. He had Marlene Dietrich on the wire for me. "Peter, angel." The famous satin voice rustled in my ear. "Have you signed Audrey Harris yet?"

"Not yet."

"Then don't. I've found the actress for you. She's marvel-ous, fantastic. That new little girl—Didi Cheri."

"But, Marlene ..."

"You know how to reach her? Of course you do. Plaza 9-0999."

"But, Marlene ..."

"Peter, *Liebchen*, I hang up now. I am in a terrible rush. I'm off to Green Hills to visit Papa! Didi Cheri ... Remember. Didi Cheri."

As I sat, rather stunned, looking at the phone, Bill Austin buzzed me again.

"Gee, Mr. Duluth, now it's Bankhead."

"Peter, darling!" Miss Bankhead's unique voice sounded in my ear. "I hear you're being dreary enough to get Audrey Harris for *Larksong*. My dear, are you out of your mind? Don't you realize you can get that divine little Didi Cheri? Peter, she's fabulously talented. She ..."

The buzzer buzzed and Bill Austin's awed voice croaked on the intercom. "She's on the other phone too."

"Who?"

"Miss Bankhead. On two phones at once! I knew that woman could do anything, but ..."

Light dawned. I said, "Put her on," and for a moment, one Miss Bankhead was gushing at my left ear about Didi Cheri while a second Miss Bankhead was asking my right ear about some vice-president at CBS. I slammed down Miss Bankhead to the left and said to the one on the right:

"Tallulah, have you heard of an actress called Didi Cheri?"

"Didi Cheri? Can anyone be called Didi Cheri? Really, darling, the very thought of it makes me retch."

"So!" I said.

I wasn't amused or intrigued or fascinated or any of the other things I was supposed to be. I was merely exasperated. Okay, so this Didi Cheri proved that she could mimic Miss Dietrich *and* Miss Bankhead *and* she had a friend in California who could sign telegrams "Danny Kaye." But if she thought she could pressure me into calling Plaza 9-0999 with these maddening stunts she was out of her mind.

THE DANNY KAYE telegram was still on my desk when Bryce Bernard came to take me to lunch. Bryce Bernard and his wife ran some sort of drama school. They had recently merged with a smalltime actor's agent called Archie Stone and now the outfit boasted the grandiloquent name of the Bernard-Stone Academy Agency. I didn't know much about Bernard, but he'd been pestering me on the phone to try out one of the Academy graduates for the small role of Stella's brother which still had to be cast, and, largely as a favor to Bill Austin—who was a Bernard-Stone client—I'd promised to case the boy.

Bryce Bernard was a big, florid, immensely self-confident man with a braying laugh who thought he had Personality. He'd been in the office only a few seconds when his never-miss-a-trick eyes fell on the telegram. Unabashedly he picked it up and whistled.

"You're not letting this fool you, are you? Danny Kaye sponsoring Didi Cheri! That would be the day!"

"You know her?"

"Know her! She was an Academy student until we threw her out. She's crazy, that one. Worse than crazy. She's dangerous!" His laugh brayed. "Last week she threatened to kill me."

"Kill you?"

"She came yelling into the office like a harpy out for my blood just because we hadn't converted her overnight into the First Lady of the Stage. A real menace. No talent, no nothing, except a colossal ego and a genius for making trouble. Whatever you do, avoid Didi Cheri like the plague."

That was all I wanted to know about Didi Cheri. When we left the office, I told Bill Austin to take all my calls from President Eisenhower personally and screen them.

Luke Little was the name of the actor Bryce Bernard was trying to sell. During lunch at Sardi's, Bernard told me how wonderful he was himself, how wonderful the Bernard-Stone Agency was, and, in passing, how wonderful Luke Little was. He seemed nervous and much too eager to please. I smelled a phony. Halfway through lunch his new partner Archie Stone showed up. I'd known Archie off and on for years before the merger. He was a sallow, mournful little man—a fairly good agent, and he always had a few pretty sound clients like Bill. That day Archie seemed as jittery as his partner, but prodded by Bernard he joined in the sales talk on Luke Little.

After lunch they took me to the Academy Agency, which was housed in a big, dreary building between 8th and 9th Avenues. Luke Little, who had a Southern accent to end all Southern accents (and looked more like a low I.Q. bull calf than an actor), was waiting in Bernard's office. I had a script of *Larksong* with me, and while we gave him a chance to glance through the part, Bernard took me upstairs to show me around the school.

It seemed the usual thing: big, drafty rehearsal rooms crowded with stage-struck kids being taught how to hit the big time by broken-down actors and actresses who'd never even hit middle time themselves. There were also smaller rooms for private lessons. Bryce Bernard pushed open the door of one of them and revealed a very handsome young man and a blonde locked in each other's arms.

The blonde saw us and disengaged herself from the young man and smiled a bland, dazzling smile at Bernard.

"Hi, darling, I was trying to loosen Gregory up in his love scenes. To him all women are Whistler's Mother." Her eyes kindled with interest. "You're Peter Duluth, aren't you? I'm Gloria Bernard, Bryce's wife." She indicated the flustered young actor. "This is Gregory Remington. You're not looking for a juvenile, are you? Gregory's got a lot on the ball."

To me, Gloria Bernard's explanation of the episode seemed perfectly on the level, not that I cared one way or the other. But Bryce Bernard's reaction was remarkable. All his grinning complacency was gone. He was literally quivering with jealous fury. The last thing I wanted was to get entangled in a family brawl, so I suggested we go hear Luke Little read.

The reading was disastrous. I've heard thousands of incompetent actors, but Luke Little topped them all. I was so mad at having been railroaded into wasting my time that I killed the reading in a couple of minutes, went into a reasonably polite "Sorry" routine, and got up. To my astonishment the oafish Luke Little turned on Bernard right in front of me.

"You told me you'd get me this part. You said it was in the bag. What sort of an agent ...?"

I hurried out of the office. Bryce Bernard hurried after me and pleaded with me to reconsider. When he saw he was only boring me, he shifted his tactics. Luke Little, he confessed, was a Texas oil heir. If I gave him the part, he'd be good for at least twenty grand to back the show. That was the end. If ever I have to hire a bad actor through a punk agency in order to raise money for a production, I bow permanently out of Broadway. I told Bryce Bernard exactly what I thought of him, of Luke Little, and of the ethics of the Bernard-Stone Academy Agency, and I strode off down the corridor.

Archie Stone was coming out of another office. I glared at him. "What's happened to you? You used to be a reputable agent."

He looked at me with a sickly smile. "You didn't like Luke?"

"Like him? I love him. I'm going to marry him." I stormed out of the building. I'd forgotten Didi Cheri, but when I got back to the office, Bill Austin handed me a list of her latest sponsors. In my absence, Bernard Baruch had called, and Greta Garbo, and Averell Harriman, and Clare Boothe Luce.

"She's fantastic." Bill's dark, intelligent face was reluctantly impressed. "I could have sworn they were all real."

The phone rang. He picked it up and listened. "No, he's not." He slammed down the receiver.

"Who is she now?" I said.

"Johnny Ray. Gee, Mr. Duluth, call Plaza 9-0999—just for the heck of it."

I withered him with a glance. "If you ever mention Didi Cheri or the Bernard-Stone Academy Agency, you're fired."

"Wasn't that actor any good? Archie was all steamed up about him."

"The very thought of him," I said, quoting Miss Bankhead, "makes me retch."

I got through what was left of the afternoon. That night I was home alone. Around ten thirty a collect call came in from Iris in Schenectady.

"Peter."

"Hi, darling. How's your mother?"

"She's fine. Peter, the most extraordinary thing happened. Mother and I met a little actress at a cocktail party this evening. I know Audrey Harris would be wonderful, but this girl is fantastic. She's Stella down to the tiniest detail. And I got her to read. Peter, you can't believe ..."

My wife is not only a fine actress, she's also the shrewdest talent spotter I know. Dubiously I said, "Who is she?"

"It's a rather unusual name. I can't think why we haven't heard of it before. It's Didi ..."

Fury clutched me by the throat. That little monster! She'd read about Iris's Schenectady visit in the columns; she'd even imitated the collect-call operator. I yelled into the mouthpiece:

"Listen, you. If you ever dare to call me here or at the office or at any other telephone number in the entire universe, I'll have you slapped in jail. I'll have you deported. I'll have you ..."

"But, darling," came the uncannily exact replica of my wife's voice, "what on earth's got into you? I ..."

"No," I said slowly, "I won't slap you in jail. I won't deport you. I'll kill you."

THAT, IT SEEMED, was the end of Didi Cheri. For two days I didn't hear a word from her. I didn't hear a word from Audrey Harris, either, but I cast the brother role easily enough without benefit of the Bernard-Stone Agency. On the third evening, about eleven thirty, Bill Austin arrived at the apartment with a cable, looking glum.

"I thought I'd break it to you myself. Mr. Duluth. I stopped by at the office and the cable had come in from England. Audrey Harris can't make it. She has a movie commitment."

I was plunged in gloom. You could count on the fingers of one hand the actresses young and talented enough to play Stella. Desperately I put in a call to Claire Bloom in London but they couldn't locate her. Just as I canceled the call the door buzzer sounded. Bill went to answer it. I heard an angry female voice in the hall and then a small, dark girl I had never laid eyes on before swept into the living room. She looked absurdly young, about fifteen; she wore her hair in a ponytail, and she was seething with rage.

"You!" Huge gray eyes blazed at me. "Aren't you ashamed? Of course you're not ashamed. Fame has destroyed all your humanity. You're Nero, that's what you are. *Two hours* I waited in that dark, dreary, empty theater."

"And who do you think ...?"

"You dare to pretend you don't know me? When you called me this evening? When you made that date for me to read for you at the Vandolan Theater at nine thirty? I suppose you thought it was funny—to raise my hopes and then dash them to the ground to punish me just because I made all those calls which any girl trying to get ahead would have done ..."

A copy of the script of *Larksong* lay on the couch. She saw it and leaped to it. Bill Austin hurried toward her.

"Hi, you!"

"Shut up," she said. "Shut up—both of you. You asked for it and you're going to get it, whether you want to or not. Shut up—and listen to Didi Cheri."

She'd picked at random one of Stella's long speeches in the second act. It was incredible. She couldn't have even seen the script before, but instantly as she started to read she was Stella. No talent—that's what Bryce Bernard had said about Didi Cheri. No talent! Bill and I looked at each other bemusedly.

When she finished the speech, Bill crossed to cue her. She went through the whole scene. It was the most extraordinary phenomenon I'd ever witnessed.

"So!" She glared at me. "I was good, wasn't I? I was terrific. Do I get the part?"

My spirits were soaring. "Yes," I said, "you get the part."

All the challenge went out of her face. She looked about eleven years old and terrified. I thought she was going to faint.

"You mean that?"

"I mean it."

"W-what about Audrey Harris?"

"She can't make it. She's tied up."

"Gee!" she breathed. "The most wonderful moment of my life! It's come at last. When do we go into rehearsal?"

"Any day now."

She smiled wanly. "I hated doing it like this, Mr. Duluth. Barging in, yelling. So unladylike. But I knew it was my only hope. And you're to blame anyway."

"Blame?"

"For calling me to read and standing me up. That's when it happened."

"When what happened?"

"The murder," she said. "That's why you've got to explain to the police if you want me in your play. There's a dead man lying in my apartment. If you don't do something, I'll be arrested."

My spirits weren't soaring any more. Crazy! Bryce Bernard had said that too. Okay, the incredible Didi Cheri was a fantastic actress, but what good was she to me if she was also out of her mind?

"Listen," I said. "Enough's enough. You pestered me with those phony calls. You accuse me of standing you up. You know I never called you tonight and ..."

"You never called me?"

"Of course I didn't."

"But you're my alibi! Oh," she said desperately, "oh, I see. It was a deliberate plot to get me out of the apartment so they could murder him there and blame it on me."

"Listen ..." I began.

"For pity's sake, stop saying listen." Her eyes were blazing again. "Don't you see how important this is? When I broke into your apartment, I was determined to get to play Stella. That's what I want more than anything in the world and I realized you'd never give me the part if you knew about—about the body. But I thought it'd be all right. I thought after I'd shown you what a terrific actress I am and you needed me, you could just explain to the police that I had nothing to do with it, that I was waiting for you at the theater, but now ..."

Tears were rolling down her cheeks. She was so extraordinary a girl that I hadn't the faintest idea whether they were genuine or not. And I figured that she probably didn't know, either.

"I went home from the theater," she moaned. "I saw Bryce Bernard lying there. I came right here to you. I thought ..."

"Bryce Bernard!" I exclaimed. "You seriously claim that Bryce Bernard ..."

"Oh, dear." Still whimpering, she stamped her foot. "Oh, dear, oh, dear, don't you listen to a word I say?"

"And you haven't called the police?"

"Of course I haven't. The moment I saw him, I came straight here."

I glanced at Bill. He started to speak and then shrugged helplessly.

"If you're making this up ..." I began.

"Making it up! Can't you see I'm telling the truth? Don't you realize my reading would have been a hundred times better if I hadn't been upset and terrified and jittery because there was a body ... ?"

I glanced at Bill again. Suddenly I had made up my mind. Young actresses like Didi Cheri happen only once in a century. Mad or not mad, and even if, incredibly, Bryce Bernard was lying dead in her apartment, I was going to have her for *Larksong*. I grabbed her arm.

"Come on," I said.

She lived on the Lower East Side in a decrepit old house of small stores and obscure offices. Her cold-water flat was on the top floor. In the taxi I'd remembered that Bryce Bernard had said she'd threatened to kill him. I tried to put that thought out of my mind. But I couldn't after we'd arrived. Because Bryce Bernard was there all right.

His big, overfed body was sprawled across the floor of the bleak little living room, his head bashed in by an andiron which lay blood-stained at his side.

WE ALL GAZED down at the body. "You see?" said Didi Cheri in an attempt at an I-told-you-so voice. She looked as if she were going to be ill. So did Bill.

He said, "I guess we call the police."

"No," said Didi Cheri passionately.

"Why not?"

"Because they'll arrest me. And if I'm arrested, how can I be in the play?" She swung round to me. "You can't get Audrey Harris. You know there's no one but me. I'm wonderful. I'll be a star overnight. I'll make you a fortune." In a lightning switch she became forlornly, irresistibly, the Damsel in Distress. "Oh, Mr. Duluth, please, *please*, do something. You see, it's not just that he's here. Last week, in front of three witnesses, I threatened to kill him."

At least she'd admitted it. I turned my back on the corpse. Bryce Bernard had not been my favorite male, but it wasn't nice to look at him. Nothing at all was pleasant any more. "Let's hear it," I said.

"He was a crook. The whole Academy Agency's a filthy racket. They get kids from out of town, kids like me crazy to be on the stage. They take all their money, as advance commissions. They're supposed to teach them and get them jobs. Teach them! You should get a load of those lessons. And you should get a load of some of the students. Any decent agency would tell them they'd never be able to act in a million years, but the Academy Agency just takes their money and keeps stalling on getting them jobs, saying they're not ready. I came to New York with three thousand dollars. I gave them two thousand. That was eight months ago and they never even landed me a TV audition. Last week I got disgusted. I went to the office. I told Bryce Bernard what I thought of him and demanded my money back."

"And what did he do?"

"He just laughed. That made me madder. I'm terrible, you know, when I'm mad. I said if I ever set eyes on him again I'd bash his head in. I swore I'd get that *Larksong* part without any help from him. I swore it. That's why I pestered you so much. I was going to get it—if only to show Bryce Bernard."

She sounded convincing—which, of course, didn't mean a thing. But everything she'd said about the Academy Agency checked with my own impression; and Bryce Bernard's attempt to warn me against her could easily have been motivated by spite, just because she'd had the guts to stand up to him.

I glanced at Bill. I hadn't hired him through the agency; I'd hired him because he'd done a good job for another producer who'd recommended him. But he *was* a Bernard-Stone client.

"Is this true about the agency, Bill?"

He was watching Didi Cheri dubiously. "It could be, I guess. I don't know a thing about the Bernards and the Academy angle. I was Archie Stone's client before the merger, and Archie's always been on the level with me."

"Oh, they *do* have regular, established clients," broke in Didi Cheri. "Of course they do. But that's only a front. The main thing, the thing they make their disgusting fortune on, is those poor kids. And when, they get someone good like me they don't even have enough sense to exploit them! Oh, Mr. Duluth, don't you see? It's one of them.

They're all crooks. Dog eat dog. One of them wanted to get rid of Mr. Bernard, and by threatening to kill him and swearing I'd land the *Larksong* part, I gave them the perfect chance to frame me. They sent me off on that wild goose chase and then they lured him down here. They didn't realize I'd go running to you. They thought I'd just get back from the theater and find the body and call the police and then, when I'd told them about you calling me to read and you'd denied it ... oh, dear, oh, dear."

I was painfully torn in two directions. The magic, the enormous excitement, of having found my Stella was still there. But another part of me was sensible enough to realize how shamelessly this exasperating little girl had been pushing me around. What proof was there that she hadn't killed Bryce Bernard and merely invented the fantastic Vandolan story to save her own skin?"

I said, "If you were at the Vandolan Theater, how did Bryce Bernard get into this apartment?"

"Oh, I've already figured that out. When I made that scene at the agency, I got so mad I forgot my purse. I left it there with a key in it. I had another key and I was darned if I'd demean myself by going back to pick up the purse. So any of them could have taken the key, let themselves in, and called Mr. Bernard from here."

"At the Vandolan, did you wait in the theater itself or in the little alley that's right outside the stage door?"

"In the theater. When I got there, the stage door was open but no one was around. Later, when I left, the stage door had been locked. I had to get out through one of the exits in the house."

"So no one saw you?"

"No one at all."

That was hopeless from the police point of view, but it sounded plausible enough. I knew the Vandolan stage-door man. When there was nothing much doing, he spent most of the evening drinking beer in an 8th Avenue spot and usually closed up around eleven. I'd told him I wouldn't be using the theater that night anyway, and it was like him not to bother to search the place before locking up.

All my instincts for self-preservation warned me to call the police, but theatrical enthusiasm and greed got the better of them. Now I'd found her, it would be disastrous for *Larksong* to have Didi Cheri languishing in the Tombs, and certainly she'd be held if we brought the police in now. Okay, I'd gamble on her. There was a chance that she was telling the truth and that one of those dubious characters at the Academy Agency had framed her.

I said, "Who was in the office when you threatened Bernard?"

"Archie Stone and Mrs. Bernard and some dopey Southern actor who was in the clutches. Luke Little is his name."

"Luke Little!"

The phone rang. We all started. It went on ringing. I said to Didi Cheri, "Answer it," and then, changing my mind, answered it myself in a gruff, indistinguishable tone. I recognized Archie Stone's voice at once although it was hoarse and rattled. Was this Plaza 9-0999? Was Bryce Bernard there? He had to talk to him. It was very important.

I said, "What makes you think there's anyone named Bernard here?"

"He left a note for me at the office. I only just found it. It says Peter Duluth called at nine thirty and wanted to see him about a *Larksong* casting. He left this number. I know it's late. But he had a date with me for ten. I waited and waited at home and then finally I went down to the office and found the note."

"Hold on a minute," I said.

I cupped the receiver, thinking fast. At least, if Archie Stone was telling the truth, we knew now how they'd got Bernard down here. They'd used me as a bait, the way they'd used me with Didi Cheri.

Back into the phone, I said, "Sorry to have kept you waiting. They say Bryce Bernard was here, but he and Mr. Duluth just left. If you want him, he should be at Mr. Duluth's in about half an hour."

I gave my home address. Archie Stone gasped, "Thanks. Thanks a lot."

He hung up. I explained to the others what I had done. This way at least I had a chance to scare the daylights out of Archie Stone.

Didi Cheri begged to go with me, but she'd filled her quota of troublemaking for one night. Bill said he had an apartment in the East Fifties and his number was in the book. I told him to take Didi Cheri there and wait till I called, then we walked out on Bryce Bernard and took two taxis.

I hadn't been home more than five minutes when the door buzzer sounded. Archie Stone, looking like a dapper and agitated mouse, scurried in.

I'd decided on my tactics in the cab. I gave him a drink and then gave him what-for. I said Bryce Bernard had been murdered, that the Academy Agency was crooked, and that he, Archie Stone, had obviously murdered Bernard to get full control of the racket. I'd never seen a more terrified man. He started babbling incoherently. Sure, the Academy Agency was a racket, but he hadn't dreamed of it when Bernard negotiated the merger. He'd only got wise after some little actress called Didi Cheri had made scene in the office. Ever since then he'd been trying to get Bernard to cancel the merger.

"I'm legitimate, Mr. Duluth. Bernard only fixed the merger to get a respectable front. I don't fit into a setup like that. You saw how it was the other day with that Luke Little. I knew he was hopeless as an actor, but Bryce made me boost him to you just because he'd given Bryce ten grand to get him on the stage and was beginning to be suspicious and demand results. You've got to believe me. All I've been trying to do is to get out from under. Just this evening I picked up the cancellation papers from the lawyers. Here!"

He fumbled a large envelope out of his pocket. "Bryce promised to sign tonight. That's why I've been so crazy to locate him. Look at them; read them. Bryce gave me five grand for the use of my name, but I already paid the money back yesterday. Those papers cancel the merger. The school's been cleaning up; it's made a fortune; but I never got a cent of that dough, merger or no merger. If Bryce is dead, the whole works goes to Gloria."

I looked through the papers. They seemed on the level. They uncompromisingly stated that Archie Stone had paid back the five thousand and thereby invalidated the merger. Almost certainly that let Archie out—that and the obvious fact that he was too craven to kill a chipmunk, let alone bash his partner's head in.

"But I still don't get it, Mr. Duluth." He had swallowed his drink and was eyeing me desperately. "How do you know Bryce is murdered? Where is he? At that number— Plaza 9-0999? That's where he was. Somebody ..."

"If you know what's good for you," I said, "don't ask questions, just play this my way. What about Little? You said Bernard chiseled ten thousand out of him and Little got wise to the racket?"

"Sure. After you'd turned him down for *Larksong*, he had a terrific fight with Bryce. But Little can't have killed him."

"Why not?"

"He gave up. He quit. Day before yesterday he flew back to Texas. It can't be Gloria, either. All evening Gloria's been with me at my place—ever since eight o'clock. She was still there when I went down to the office at twelve thirty."

I was starting to feel a most peculiar and unpleasant sensation. Only three people could have framed Didi Cheri in just the way she'd been framed, and all three of them, for one reason or another, seemed to be eliminated. Had I, then, been played for the original sucker after all? Had that brash, talented, impossible little ...

I glared at Archie Stone. "What was Gloria Bernard doing at your place?"

"I needed her. Bryce didn't want to sign the cancellation. I was working it through Gloria."

"She wanted it signed?"

"No. She didn't either, but I've got Gloria where I want her and she knows it." He gave a sickly grin. "In the jealousy department, Bryce makes Othello look like Bo-peep, and I happened to know Gloria's got a heavy boy friend. She hates Bryce's guts; she'd have left him months ago if it weren't for the dough. She's money-mad."

Excitement started to stir in me. The shrewd, blasé Gloria Bernard, who "loosened up" young actors in the rehearsal rooms, had a boy friend; with Bryce dead she inherited full control of the crooked Academy. That was more than enough motive for her—but what about the boy friend? She could have given him Didi Cheri's key, had him imitate me on the phone, and masterminded the whole murder frame-up by remote control.

I said, "Who's her boy friend? One of the Academy students?"

"Maybe." Archie blinked. "She's far too smart to let on."

"Then how do you know she has one?"

"I caught her a couple of times making phone calls. And then, once when Bryce was in L.A. and she was expecting a late call from a London agency, she gave me a number where they could reach her overnight. Sick aunt, she said! I just laughed and she had to admit it was a boy friend, but she made me swear not to tell Bryce."

"You remember this number?"

"I couldn't forget it. It's the one hold I've had on her to force her into helping me break the merger. It's Wilton 7-0202."

I scribbled the number down. My excitement was mounting. "Okay," I said. "That's all. Now get out of here."

"But, Mr. Duluth ..."

"Get out, and if you breathe a word of this to Gloria Bernard, I'll see you're hounded off Broadway once and for all."

A few moments after he'd scurried out, the phone rang. It was Didi Cheri, this time as herself for a change.

"Oh, Mr. Duluth, I can't bear the suspense. What's happening?"

"Where are you?"

"At a drug store down the block. I couldn't stay with Bill. He's sweet, but a girl can't just sit staring hopelessly at a sweet boy when her whole life's at stake. I asked for a glass of milk and ran out when he was in the kitchen."

Suddenly I saw what we had to do. "Come here this instant."

"With the speed of light," said Didi Cheri.

Soon she came running in, her ponytail bobbing, her eyes shining. I told her my hunch about Gloria Bernard and her boy friend.

"With any luck you can work it," I said.

"Me?"

"You can imitate Marlene Dietrich and Tallulah Bankhead and Bernard Baruch; it's a cinch you can imitate Gloria Bernard. Call Wilton 7-0202. Whoever answers, make like Gloria Bernard. Say you and I have just been to see her; say we've discovered Bryce is murdered; say we realize you've been framed, but say you blurted out you'd just remembered you'd left something—your gloves—on the stage at the Vandolan. Explain that the gloves will prove you really were there and give you an alibi. Explain that the only way to keep the frame-up sticking is for him to rush right around to the Vandolan and pick them up before we get there. Also say you babbled something about leaving by a house exit, which means it'll still be open because they don't close from the outside."

"Gee!" said Didi Cheri. "And we'll be waiting there. We'll catch him red-handed. That'll fix them both. Of course it will."

"If she hasn't already got in touch with him," I said. "But there's a good chance she hasn't. If she's as smart as I think, she'll have enough sense to steer very clear of him until her alibi's solid with the police."

Didi Cheri made a spring for the telephone.

"Not here," I said. "We don't know where the boy friend lives. Maybe he's closer to the theater than we are. Come on."

We took a cab to the theater district and squeezed together into a telephone booth in an all-night drug store. Didi Cheri dialed the number. A man answered. Taut as a wire, I listened to her extraordinary imitation of Gloria Bernard's sexy New York drawl. For a moment I thought she was overdoing it, but she wasn't. As she delivered the message, I could hear the man's voice, hoarse with nerves, crackling into the earpiece. "No, oh, no! ... Yes, of course." She slammed down the receiver and wriggled around to face me.

"It worked. It's both of them—Gloria Bernard and the boy friend. This has got them—utterly."

"Quick," I said. "Let's get out of here."

We hurried to the Vandolan. We had almost reached it when we passed a cop on the corner. Didi Cheri spun around.

"A police witness! That's just what we need."

She ran back to the cop and started gabbling. He hadn't, I'm sure, the slightest idea what she was talking about, but Didi Cheri, with her sublime combination of indignation, helplessness, and mystification, was as much a match for him as she had been for me. In a couple of minutes she had him following meekly behind us like a tame bear.

We found the house exit by which Didi Cheri had left. It was on the alley leading to the stage door. We slipped through it into the dark theater, leaving it obviously ajar to guide the "boy friend." The policeman had a flashlight. We hurried down the center aisle. The Vandolan has no orchestra pit. I dropped Didi Cheri's white gloves center stage near the edge under the proscenium. Didi Cheri dragged the policeman through the seats into a dark corner behind a column. I lay down on the floor between the first two rows of orchestra seats on the center aisle, the most strategic place from which to jump the "boy friend" when—and if—he picked up the gloves.

I tried to make Didi Cheri join the cop but failed miserably. She lay down behind the seats across the aisle from me, peering tensely at the stage.

"Soon I'll be there," she whispered. "People will be screaming, shouting, bravoing, applauding. Bouquets will be tossed."

"Either that," I said, "or you'll be rotting in jail."

That shut her up. I lay there in the familiar, dusty theater darkness, trying to figure out how I'd managed to let myself be railroaded into doing so improbable a thing. My eyes had become accustomed to the gloom. By peering around the edge of the aisle seat, I could see the gloves gleaming faintly under the proscenium. Hours seemed to pass, but I suppose they were only minutes. Didi was so quiet I thought she must have slipped away. And then, just as the suspense was becoming intolerable, I heard behind me the faint clanging sound of the exit door being pulled outward. I stiffened. There was a scuffle, a muffled exclamation as if someone had stumbled, and then, very softly, footsteps seemed to start padding down the center aisle.

They were hurrying, almost running. In a couple of seconds they were right up to us, and as I held my breath, I could make out the shadowy shape of legs passing within inches of me. The footsteps went on toward the stage. As I peered around the edge of the seat, a flashlight sprang on. I saw its beam cruise the stage and settle on the gloves. I saw the man scramble onto the stage and bend to pick them up.

Didi Cheri was quicker than I. With a piercing scream of "Help, cops!" she dashed down the aisle, vaulted up onto the stage, and threw herself on the man. As I rushed to join them, he flung her off and sprang to the left. That was when I tackled him. We both went down onto the bare boards of the stage and Didi Cheri, still yelling, jumped on top of both of us.

For a moment all was hopeless confusion; then the cop came lumbering up. The man who had picked up the gloves was writhing under me. The cop's flashlight beam caught both our faces. It blinded me for a moment and it was Didi Cheri who gasped, "Bill Austin!"

I could recognize the man's face then. It was Bill Austin's and it was white and distorted with frustrated fury. For a moment I merely felt stupefied; then it all began to fit. I'd only just hired Bill. I hadn't known a thing about him. If I'd looked him up in the book, I'd have known his telephone number was Wilton 7-0202, but I hadn't. And he was a Bernard-Stone client. I should have guessed that he could have been Gloria Bernard's young man just as well as anyone else, and, with him working for me, the two of them had been in the ideal position to stage the murder. They knew the whole Didi Cheri setup from my end as well as the Academy's. After Bill Austin had killed Bryce Bernard, he'd deliberately stopped by at my place with the Audrey Harris cable to be on hand if anything went wrong. The nerve of it! As I kept him, still struggling, pinioned to the stage, indignation took the place of astonishment.

"Okay." The cop's hand was on my shoulder. "Break it up. Whatever this is, straighten it out at the precinct house."

I scrambled to my feet. Bill Austin got up too.

"Hold him, officer," shouted Didi Cheri. "He's dangerous. He's a murderer. And there's another one, an accomplice, a female ..."

"Okay, lady, okay."

The cop closed a huge hand around Bill Austin's arm. It was over. My tactics had been chancy and Didi Cheri-ish in the extreme, but, like the incomparable Didi Cheri herself, they had succeeded.

We all started down the aisle toward the exit. The cop's flashlight beam, moving at random, rested for a second on Didi Cheri's face. It was ecstatic now, Joan of Arc listening to her voices.

"We've made it!" she breathed. "I get to play Stella after all. Think of it! Didi Cheri in *Larksong*. Huge neon letters blazing across the marquee. Didi Cheri ..."

The producer in me was beginning to re-emerge. "Where, for pity's sake, did you get that name?"

"What's wrong with it? It's the one thing the Academy Agency gave me. Didi Cheri in *Lark* ..."

"What's your real name?"

"Dorothy," she said. "Dorothy Gubbins."

"Okay," I said. "In the neon light department, read Dorothy Gubbins."

"But, Mr. Duluth, how can anybody be glamorous when they're called—?"

"With what you've got," I said, "you could be called Pickleburger and be as glamorous as Dietrich, Bankhead, and Garbo all put together."

"Gee, Mr. Duluth, you really mean that?"

"I mean it."

"Gee!" said Dorothy Gubbins, the rising young actress.

And we followed the cop and one of Bryce Bernard's murderers out of the darkened theater.

Postscript: Puzzle for Proustians

Concerning the adventures of young Richard "Rickie" Webb in Paris, Maurice-Bernard Endrébe (1918-2005), a prominent crime writer and critic who translated many of the Patrick Quentin novels into French, related an amusing anecdote in the twelfth chapter of his novel *La Vieille Dame sans Merci* (1952). Around 1920, it seems, Webb—in the novel generally referred to as an "English friend"—spent his holiday in France. In a Parisian salon with literary pretensions, he was introduced as a "very nice boy" to a man with a pale forehead and a wisp of black hair: Marcel Proust. Appreciating that he had met one of the great writers of the twentieth century, Webb immediately tried to locate the literary legend's complete works. From a Parisian bookseller he bought about twenty volumes, for which he paid almost one hundred francs, and that very evening started perusing them. Sadly, his first approach to Proust was a grave disappointment.

A couple of weeks later, young Rickie was in Cannes, a guest of some friends, and he spoke of his disappointing experience with the great Proust's novels. His friends were all astonished, because Webb was considered a highly intelligent and cultivated person. When his landlady said she had been a devotee of Proust since reading the first pages of *Du coté de chez Swann*, Webb replied: "Ah, I had asked for all the complete works of Proust, but they didn't give me this book!"

Upon having *Du coté de chez Swann* lent him, Webb immediately started reading the novel, becoming absorbed by it immediately. Thrilled beyond all description, he stayed awake the entire night to complete the book. Later, when speaking to the woman who had lent him the book, Webb innocently declared that he found the *Duchesse de Guermantes* much more aristocratic than the *Princesse d'Erminge*. With that observation what might be termed *The Proust Puzzle* was solved! Rickie Webb surely was one of the few people in the world to have read a score of novels by Marcel *Prévost* without realizing it at the time.

Mauro Boncompagni
Genova, Italy

Afterword on Hugh Wheeler

All through my childhood, my great-uncle, Hugh Wheeler, remained a mysterious figure. The only brother of my grandfather, Jack, Hugh had set out for New York from London when he was twenty-one and seemed to have only returned to England on rare occasions ever since. I knew he was a writer, however, because a shelf of my grandfather's bookcase was dedicated to a sizeable collection of his detective stories written, confusingly, under a trio of pseudonyms.

My grandfather was a raconteur and I was an attentive listener to his tales. The more he enjoyed telling a story, the more often he would repeat it—so some of his anecdotes I got to know very well. Because Hugh and Jack were close as boys and as young men, Hugh figured largely in these narratives. He played a crucial part, for example, in a story that haunted my childhood: a story of the two brothers hiking over the boggy landscape of Dartmoor and seeking shelter from the winter wind in a convenient hollow. Unscrewing the lid of their thermos flasks, each sitting in a different corner of the dell, they independently felt a radical, inexplicable dread and each looked up to see the other, ashen–faced, staring at his brother — before they fumbled with their belongings and fled. The uncanniness of this story made it impossible to forget (my grandfather narrated the occurrence in a serious tone and never tried to explain it) — but in fact the background premise of the story — the brothers' liking for companionable hikes together—was part of a pattern of less eventful activity that suggests a wide sharing of interests. They both spent time on a remote island called Skomer, off the Welsh coast, helping to ring migrating seabirds, and both were attracted, all their lives, to wild places and to the animals and birds that lived there.

Then, too, they shared a common history of family and school. I never met my great grandfather, Harold, or my

great grandmother, Florence, but they have been identified — in a rather fulsome letter from Jack and Hugh's
headmaster — as providing for their boys 'that inestima-
ble blessing...a good God-fearing English home.' Judging
from the frequency with which that head teacher needed
to respond to Florence's earnest epistles about her sons,
she seems to have been the main decision-maker in the
boys' early lives. She must have been a woman of firm
opinions. My grandfather would recall, wonderingly,
that his mother had chosen their preparatory school sole-
ly because, at the local bus stop, she took a liking to the
way its boys doffed their little caps. It is not as clear why
she chose their boarding school, but their time there is
well-documented in the copious correspondence sent by
the head master to their indefatigable mother. Although
the brothers were three years apart, Hugh's academic
precocity propelled him, within a few months of arrival
at this school, into the same class as his older brother.
My grandfather acknowledged without a trace of ran-
cour that Hugh was his intellectual superior, but many
decades later still shuddered about the embarrassment he
felt when they were briefly in the same class and sighed
with relief that Hugh was, mercifully soon advanced to a
higher class.

From this shared history, their lives took divergent paths.
My grandfather, advised by his school that—unlike his
brother—his virtues were more sound than brilliant, became
an accountant, got married, started a family and moved to a
thatched cottage in a small village in Devon. Hugh moved
from university in London to the United States, became the
collaborator there for the detective fiction of a fellow Englishman whom my grandfather referred to only as 'Rickie,' with
a note of reproach for having lured his brother away from
England. About twenty years later, Hugh went on to write
plays, soon inhabiting a heady world of famous actors and
actresses that must have seemed very distant from a cottage
(complete with dilapidated blacksmith's forge) in Devon.

Hugh did, however, use this cottage on occasion as a refuge from the demands of that theatrical world and visit my grandparents, apparently appreciative of the tranquillity that their contrasting world offered. Over breakfast, he would proffer calmly, to my startled grandfather, the occasional postcard from Laurence Olivier and Vivien Leigh (signed, according to my grandfather, just 'Larry and Viv'), thus unwittingly underscoring the distance between the brothers' two planes of existence.

This wide distance between the English provinces and Broadway had, however, been traversed by my grandfather's oldest son, my uncle John, who had been sent to New York at the age of twenty-one to stay with Hugh. In an episode John himself would often recount with self-deprecating relish, he was taken to a Broadway performance of one of Hugh's plays, and when treated to a surprise introduction to Noel Coward, disgraced himself by holding out a callow hand and asking brightly, 'So, what do you do?' Uncle John accredits—rationally, perhaps—this disastrous social encounter with an increased distance between Hugh and his family in England.

I was the next to try to bridge that gap when I was invited to New York by an American (the man I subsequently married). I wrote—prompted by the optimism of youth—to my grandfather, straightaway, to see if he could arrange for me to meet this his elusive brother. I still have the letter that Hugh wrote to me, suggesting how we could meet. The letter set clear limits on the family feeling to which I might have tried to claim — but does this graciously: 'I have never had really any family feeling (largely through leaving home very young) so it's practically impossible for me to know how to play the role of uncle (great uncle) and suspect I wouldn't excel at it. So when we meet it should be as two people who would or would not like each other as any old human beings.' This clear limitation on the kind of familial connection I might have expected served me well. I wrote enthusiastic letters expressing my excitement about coming to New York, while carefully avoiding expressing any specific expectations of how he would respond. He wrote back — a little guardedly at first, and then with more certainty and ease.

The meeting itself turned out to be difficult to arrange because he was not often in New York. Hugh spent his winters in the Caribbean, in an apartment on St Kitts, and much of the rest of the year in his eighteenth-century clapboard house in Massachusetts, only coming to New York, I think, for specific work commitments. At the time that I first contacted him, the Spring of 1980, these mostly seemed to involve the writing of books for musicals and scripts for films. He was then in the third stage of his literary self-re-invention — after three decades of writing detective fiction followed by a switch to play–writing in the early sixties. His first letters to me reported the variable critical receptions to *Sweeney Todd*, in New York, London and Washington and the progress he was making on a movie script involving Soviets (I think it must have been *Nijinsky*). It seems fitting therefore that the sole contact that my first approach triggered from him was in the mediated form of a performance of *Sweeney Todd* in New York, from which he was absent but for which he kindly left me tickets.

It was not until the summer of 1980 that I finally met him. He was living on East 55th Street in an apartment which he had taken over from Noel Coward. We met in the apartment before going to dinner in a restaurant nearby. I remember the strange juxtaposition of exotic and familiar: it seemed surreal to be walking through an apartment where Noel Coward had eaten his breakfast and brushed his teeth — but I would sometimes catch an expression or a movement of countenance that exactly replicated responses I had thought unique to my grandfather. We talked over dinner. He told us about his various writing projects (he was rehearsing with the New York City Opera the Kurt Weill opera, *Silverlake*, for which he had written a new script). I explained to him that I was considering following his footsteps and moving from London to America. I was going into my final year of studying English Literature at Cambridge and was thinking of applying to graduate school in New York: I had a general sense of his approval of my plans. I also saw that he had a writer's alertness for material: he would point out interesting characters around us, at neighbouring tables, and flag up intriguing scraps of conversation he overheard.

This categorisation of people according to their potential as fiction seemed to extend to his family. During dinner I chatted about various of his relatives and found that he had the haziest knowledge of their kinship to him. He seemed to make no distinction between people to whom he was related and those who were not: at one time he expressed an enthusiastic hope that he might have a blood tie to a particularly colourful character (whose eccentricities I was describing) and was entirely unperturbed to find out that he did not. He was especially struck by my proud purchase earlier that day, in the stacks of a celebrated New York second-hand bookstore, of a volume about *The Sexual Reproduction of Snails*. I explained that my mother was a keen keeper of large Roman Snails and had great difficulty encouraging them to mate (their double set of sexual organs makes successful copulation a challenge): this book would be an invaluable guide for her. In subsequent letters, he would refer back to this purchase and ask with interest about my mother—whom he evidently saw as an entirely fantastical figure — and her careful nurture of the creatures that he insisted on labelling her 'Giant Slugs.'

The year after I met my great uncle, I became a graduate student at Columbia University and moved to New York. There, taking careful heed of his initial warning, I wrote to him regularly (keeping him posted about the various relatives he seemed to enjoy as fictional characters); accepted with gratitude tickets to his shows and occasional meals out; and received ever warmer letters from him, telling me about the birds and animals he had seen in the grounds of his Massachusetts home and the writing he was then doing.

Still sensitised to the possibility that my presence in the country — which I always thought he must have chosen as a sanctuary from more confining English mores and values— might seem intrusive, I was glad to receive an unexpected seal of approval. At one time, in the four years I lived in New York, I was visited by my Uncle John (he of the Noel Coward debacle) and Hugh civilly spent an afternoon accompanying us—and John's teenage children—on a tourist boat that circumnavigated Manhattan. When we said goodbye, there was a noticeable look of relief on his face (he had performed his familial duty and could return with a good conscience to the life he preferred)—but just before I turned away he clasped my hands warmly and asked me emphatically to keep sending him my letters.

When I moved back to England, I kept on writing to him and when, a few years later, he died, I found that I had been remembered with startling generosity as a beneficiary. Like the bonds between characters in so many of the eighteenth-century novels in the university classes that I now taught, ours was essentially an epistolary relationship—but that didn't diminish its importance to me. His death was a sadness and a loss. Out of respect, however, for one who seemed so determined a maintainer of privacy from his family, I confined myself to reading the obituaries with attentive pride and restrained from trying to fill in the large gaps in my knowledge about Hugh's life. I was even a hesitant reader of his work, worried that this might count as an invasion of his privacy (though I was always a deeply grateful recipient for the tickets that increasingly came my way to the musicals whose books he had written—*A Little Night Music, Candide* and *Sweeney Todd* — attending each performance with rapt attention).

As the years have gone on, however, I have found that my curiosity has increased as my sense of the inviolacy of his biographical details has softened. When the publishers of this collection of stories, therefore, asked me to write an afterword based on my personal knowledge of Hugh

Wheeler, my appetite for information felt sanctioned at last and I began to read with assiduity anything I could get my hands on.

Using the internet, I read not only obituaries but reviews, criticism and biographical speculations.... I particularly liked a piece labelled 'Forgotten Authors Number 55: Hugh Wheeler' by a writer in the English newspaper, *The Independent*. In it, Christopher Fowler acknowledged the difficulty of accessing biographical material about this 'chameleon' author: 'facts about him are hopelessly few, perhaps because he remained single and lived privately.' By 'chang[ing] names' and 'switch[ing] genres,' such writers, Fowler observes, make the task of 'tracking their work' a 'slippery business.' Indeed, this shifting among genres—so characteristic of Hugh—confused the writer of his obituary in the London *Times* (July 30, 1987) into forgetting entirely his work as a librettist and the omission had to be pointed out roundly by Hal Prince, the director of several of Hugh's plays and films, in an addendum to the obituary two or three weeks later. As for the name-changing, Mauro Boncompagni, in an article that tries to untangle from the various pseudonyms — Patrick Quentin, Q.Patrick, Jonathan Stagge—the literary collaborations behind them, quotes Douglas G. Greene's Introduction to the 1989 reprinting of the Patrick Quentin *Puzzle for Players*: the story of these 'collaborators and their pseudonyms makes almost as tangled a tale as the plots of Golden Age detective fiction.' Boncompagni, however, does succeed in clarifying Hugh Wheeler's role in this complex network of detective fiction and goes on to track his later work in theatre and in film. Noting that Alan Sinfield had credited him with 'being the playwright at this time 'who tried hardest to shift the atmosphere [regarding homosexuality] on Broadway,' he makes an implicit link with the film scripts which he calls 'remarkable for their exploration of alternative sexualities.'

In fact, Hugh Wheeler's literary and theatrical output is so wide-ranging that it is hard to fit it into any overarching theme. Behind the stellar titles of *Sweeney Todd*, *A Little Night Music* and *Candide*, there are numerous titles of shows that have faded from our vision because, perhaps, they closed in previews, like the 1981 adaptation of *The Little Prince*, or were never completed (like the adaptation of *The Merry Widow* that he was working on just before his death) or because (like *Pacific Overtures*, nominated for ten awards when it was first produced in 1976) they are now only rarely performed. His was a tireless writer's working life. Over fifty-six years he collaborated, adapted, created and rewrote.

MY RESEARCH INTO his literary output gave me a strong sense of the sustained diligence (and sheer breadth) of his writing — but it didn't give me a sense of his emergence as a writer from the life into which he had been born and from which he had sedulously distanced himself. A connecting link, however, was uncovered by me while rootling in my parents' attic. My mother had remembered that after her father had died, a neighbour had salvaged from an outbuilding (one that had been used to fatten a pig during the lean years of the Second World War) a sack of papers that had evidently been overlooked by the crew who cleared my grandfather's house in preparation for its sale. The conscientious neighbour retrieved the sack and alerted my mother; my parents duly brought it back to their house — and there it had remained ever since. I spent an afternoon sorting through the miscellaneous, faded papers from this sack and found a treasure trove of material documenting one family's life from 1917 to the time of my grandfather's death not long after Hugh's. I separated out all of the material that related to my great uncle and took it home to examine it more closely. Read through chronologically, the letters, school reports and annotated photos together charted — with variable degrees of detail — Hugh's trajectory from a small child in the First World War through his years at boarding school to his early writing life and eventual settlement in America. The inattention of the house clearance team, the diligence of the neighbour, and my mother's careful storage of the papers had given me access to the early world which Hugh had inhabited.

The earliest of these letters are from Hugh's father, Harold, to his mother, Florence. In 1917, an officer in the First World War and living away from his young family, he writes that he looks 'forward hopefully to the future when I shall have done with my war and you with your *little* children and we shall be free to look after one another again.' Despite referring to Hugh (now five) and Jack (eight) as 'those two lumps' he seems to have been a fond father, asking Florence to '[t]ell Jack and Hugh that all caterpillars are turning into chrysalises for the winter and are quite safe.'

Among all the papers deposited in the sack, by far the richest chronicle is that of Hugh's time at boarding school. This school, Clayesmore, had been founded by Hugh's head master, Alex Devine, an interesting character who had written several books about education (including a 1910 work, *A Crisis in the Education of the Governing Classes in England*) as well as campaigning energetically for Montenegrin independence. Hugh was sent to Clayesmore in 1925, at the age of thirteen, to join his brother Jack (soundly endorsed by Devine as a 'good type of jolly English boy'). Devine's insistence that Hugh was soon 'getting into his stride at his new school' is belied by a pitiful letter from Hugh, telling his mother that he is 'not at all setteled down[sic]' and 'Everything is in a rush.' The school, he writes, 'doesn't seem as nice as I thought it would be' and he signs the letter, 'Yours terribly lovingly, Hugh.'

Within eight months of Hugh's arrival, however, Devine had identified him as 'full of promise' — and a year after that he wrote a congratulatory letter to Hugh's mother: 'Young Hugh, in the Lower Certificate, has done splendidly.' From this time on, Hugh seems to have been specifically marked out by Devine as a future source of reflected glory for the school. Devine wrote of Hugh as a boy 'with some distinction, and just the type of boy for a scholarship [for Oxford or Cambridge].'

In the face of doubts expressed by Hugh's father, Devine points out that a scholarship at Oxford or Cambridge 'would lead naturally to the First Class of the Civil Service and do for the boy much more than anything else could.' By the time of Hugh's sixteenth birthday, Devine's letters betray increasing awareness that Hugh was not going to be as accommodating of the school's vision for him as Devine had hoped. Hugh seems to have rejected the idea of his Confirmation (presumably a blow for a man who had written *The Boys' Prayer Book* in 1913) and has had to be reprimanded for infringing the schools' dress code. Of more concern seems to have been Hugh's friendship with an American boy 'who is rather foolish and precocious, as they are in America, …always talking about sweethearts …they know all the Film artistes by name and speak about them—not at all English….' When the American boy leaves Clayesmore, Devine's sigh of relief is palpable: he has come to the 'definite conclusion that the influence of that boy…was bad….'

In May 1929, just after Hugh's seventeenth birthday, his clash of values with the school came to a dramatic head. I have a letter written by Hugh, in white heat, to his father after an explosive meeting with Devine. Refusing to be 'bullied into serving penal servitude for the dear old school's sake,' Hugh makes clear his resentment that the 'Headmaster wants to wring a scholarship out of me.' Spurred on, presumably, by the same unhappy meeting, Devine declares to Hugh's father that it is a 'cruel shame that [Hugh] should not score for the school…' 'Hugh is a difficult boy,' he concedes: 'I am anxious about him … he has queer ideas and is particularly liable to outside influences that are dangerous.' As an example of this, he reveals that Hugh has 'got hold of' Aldous Huxley's *Point and Counterpoint*, a book that Devine calls 'utterly immoral.'

Hugh's father agrees with Devine about the importance of protecting his son from bad influences but defended his son's reading habits as those of the 'modern boy who seems to read everything' and to read it 'critically and analytically.' In fact, Harold took Hugh's literary ambitions sufficiently seriously to have sent off some typewritten verses to an old friend earlier that year. The friend sends warm praise for the poems: 'Hugh's verses strike me as really extraordinary.' Reading through these half dozen poetic offerings, I find myself impressed by the energy of the eighteen-year old Hugh's expression, the clarity of his observation, the skilfully crafted cadence of the lines. In a poem entitled 'There is a Story About Roses,' in the line 'The poplars sigh in dark perpetual grief,' I register with respect the way in which his juxtaposition of two sibilants has replicated the trees' sigh. Reading through these poems, Hugh's literary gifts are conspicuous and it is easy to see why Devine was so keen on using them to net an honour for the school.

Devine died a few months after Hugh left Clayesmore and therefore never knew that Hugh went on to choose the kind of life that Devine was so determined to keep him from. At some point in his degree course in English Literature at University College, London — there seem to be conflicting opinions when — Hugh met Richard Webb, who had already co-written several mystery novels, and was looking for a new collaborator. The next letter I have from the attic-stored sack is headed 'Norddeutscher Lloyd Bremen D. 'Europa' — the name of the ship on which he and Webb sailed together to New York. He writes to his mother as the 'prickly' sky line of Manhattan has just come into view. He compares the Statue of Liberty to Lady Macbeth and adds, hopefully, 'I still get on very well with Rickie.—Long may it continue.'

In a single envelope dated October 27, 1933, a letter from Hugh to his brother Jack is enclosed in a letter from Webb to Hugh's father. Hugh congratulates his brother on his impending marriage and explains that he is working 'terribly hard on a quite pretentious novel about an English family coming to America.' The 'best parts,' he enthuses candidly 'are all Rickie's.' He hopes to get work as a drama critic on a paper, but in the meantime takes seriously his writing with Webb: 'We are very hard-boiled about it all and talk out every scene for hours...' Hugh's upbeat insistence — to his brother about the viability of a writing career in America is undercut by a single admission of homesickness, triggered when he hears a starling, 'burbling as if it were on Mrs. Baker's chimney.'

The letter from Webb to Harold Wheeler is full of reassurances about Hugh's future. Calling the 'popular American market' a 'little gold mine,' Webb reports that he and Hugh are waiting to hear news about a batch of stories they sent off a week or so ago and announces that they will halve the proceeds 'as we worked about equally.' He tells Harold that he and Hugh are attending a 'very good short story class' and plan to collaborate on a novel next. Presenting himself very much as Hugh's protector and mentor, Webb finishes by declaring himself 'delighted to have Hugh stay as long as he wants' but makes it clear that he will put 'no barriers in his way when you—or he—think it advisable for him to return home.'

In a letter that must have been written a little later, Hugh asks his father to go to the American consul and find out how to get on the quota for an American work visa. He reports with glee that 'even with writing, one gets about eight times as much money for a short-story or novel here as one does in England.' The work visa must have been forthcoming because Hugh settled in America, took American citizenship and signed up to fight for America in the Second World War. In a letter to his parents, Hugh's brother, Jack, tells them not to worry that they haven't heard from Hugh: 'There are all sorts of restrictions on Anglo-American troops' mails.'

Four years after the war ended, my grandparents met Hugh and Webb for an Easter holiday in Southern Italy. An album of diminutive black and white photos show my decorous English grandmother, Betty, sitting on a Sorrento balcony, flanked by the suaver figures of Hugh and Webb. The photos record the stages of their journey through Naples and to Capri, ending with a shot of the two writers waving farewell on a Capri dock as my grandparents' ferry pulls away. It must have been about this time that Hugh sat for a studio portrait, resplendent in white suit and gleaming, brushed-back hair; his candid gaze and pearly skin radiate quiet success. The photograph, taken at Bachrach (an established set of studios responsible for photographic portraits of a plethora of luminaries including Henry Ford and Eleanor Roosevelt), and signed in bold dark ink, 'Mum and Dad, with love Hugh,' is clearly a kind of victory banner, sent to his parents as proof that the gamble he had taken — of turning his back on the safer course of a life in the hallowed professions of the English middle class—had paid off.

Hugh's transformation from English schoolboy to a successful writer who would soon be at ease with celebrities of stage and film is only partially chronicled by the serendipitously preserved papers tucked away in the pig sty. Now that I have begun to open up the narrative of that transformation, I want to know more—so having discovered that a research center in Boston University holds a large collection of Wheeler manuscripts, reviews, scrapbooks, photographs and letters, I find I am already imagining how it will feel to open up that horde of archival riches.

In the meantime, my life has been enhanced in many ways by my great uncle's talents, by his productivity and his literary range. Through the requests I receive from people all over the world who want to use his work, I can map the enduring legacy of his writing. In high schools in almost every American state, in amateur opera groups in Australia, in the English National Opera, in a repertory theatre in the Philippines, in Swedish television studios, in Italian publishing houses—and in countless other places, pedestrian and exotic—his works are endlessly performed, filmed, adapted, translated, printed. Where my grandfather had a single shelf of his brother's detective fiction, all published in America or England, I have shelves of my great uncle's books, impressive in their diversity. They include: a translation of *A Puzzle for Fools* in the bright yellow cover that is the Italian badge of a mystery novel; a Czech version of *The Wife of Ronald Sheldon*, incorporating cartoons and television stills, their speech bubbles studded with unfamiliar, angular accents; an edition of *Black Widow*, opening from the back onto vertical rows of exquisite (and, to me, incomprehensible) Korean typographic characters.... Where once I gazed with curiosity at my grandfather's shelf, I now scan with pleased recognition my collection of my great uncle's books. The multiplicity of their forms serves as a testament both to the longevity of his appeal and to the variety of audiences eager for his work.

Joanna Gondris
Twickenham
October 2015

Sources

"Death Rides the Ski-Tow," *The American Magazine*, April 1941

"Murder with Flowers," *The American Magazine*, December 1941

"Puzzle for Poppy," *Ellery Queen's Mystery Magazine*, February 1946

"Death and the Rising Star," *Better Living Magazine*, June 1955; *Ellery Queen's Mystery Magazine*, December 1957

The Puzzles of Peter Duluth

The Puzzles of Peter Duluth by Patrick Quentin, with an introduction by Curtis Evans, a Postscript by Mauro Boncompagni, and an Afterword by Joanna Gondris, is set in Palatino and printed on 60 pound Natural acid-free paper. It was published both in full cloth and in trade softcover. The cover is by Gail Cross. *The Puzzles of Peter Duluth* was printed and bound by Thomson-Shore, and published in March 2016 by Crippen & Landru Publishers, Norfolk, Virginia.

CRIPPEN & LANDRU, PUBLISHERS
P. O. Box 9315
Norfolk, VA 23505
Web: www.crippenlandru.com
E-mail:info@crippenlandru.com

Since 1994, Crippen & Landru has published more than 100 first editions of short-story collections by important detective and mystery writers.

This is the best edited, most attractively packaged line of mystery books introduced in this decade. The books are equally valuable to collectors and readers. [*Mystery Scene Magazine*]

The specialty publisher with the most star-studded list is Crippen & Landru, which has produced short story collections by some of the biggest names in contemporary crime fiction. [*Ellery Queen's Mystery Magazine*]

God Bless Crippen & Landru. [*The Strand Magazine*]

A monument in the making is appearing year by year from Crippen & Landru, a small press devoted exclusively to publishing the criminous short story. [*Alfred Hitchcock's Mystery Magazine*]

CRIPPEN & LANDRU LOST CLASSICS

Crippen & Landru is proud to publish a series of *new* short-story collections by great authors who specialized in traditional mysteries. Each book collects stories from crumbling pages of old pulp, digest, and slick magazines, and most of the stories have been "lost" since their first publication.

We have received many requests for a complete list of "Lost Classics." Only those books with prices listed below are currently in print (March 2016) but out of print books can often be found on the web or from mystery bookshops.

The Newtonian Egg and Other Cases of Rolf le Roux by Peter Godfrey, introduction by Ronald Godfrey. 2002.

Murder, Mystery and Malone by Craig Rice, edited by Jeffrey A. Marks. 2002.

The Sleuth of Baghdad: The Inspector Chafik Stories, by Charles B. Child. 2002. Trade softcover, $17.00.

Hildegarde Withers: Uncollected Riddles by Stuart Palmer, introduction by Mrs. Stuart Palmer. 2002.

The Spotted Cat and Other Mysteries from the Casebook of Inspector Cockrill by Christianna Brand, edited by Tony Medawar. 2002. Cloth, $29.00. Trade softcover, $19.00.

Marksman and Other Stories by William Campbell Gault, edited by Bill Pronzini; afterword by Shelley Gault. 2003. Trade softcover, $19.00.

Karmesin: The World's Greatest Criminal — Or Most Outrageous Liar by Gerald Kersh, edited by Paul Duncan. 2003. Cloth, $27.00

The Complete Curious Mr. Tarrant by C. Daly King, introduction by Edward D. Hoch. 2003.

The Pleasant Assassin and Other Cases of Dr. Basil Willing by Helen McCloy, introduction by B. A. Pike. 2003. Cloth, $27.00. Trade softcover, $18.00.

Murder – All Kinds by William L. DeAndrea, introduction by Jane Haddam. 2003. Cloth, $29.00.

The Avenging Chance and Other Mysteries from Roger Sheringham's Casebook by Anthony Berkeley, edited by Tony Medawar and Arthur Robinson. 2004. Second edition enlarged, 2015. Trade softcover, $19.00.

Banner Deadlines: The Impossible Files of Senator Brooks U. Banner by Joseph Commings, edited by Robert Adey; memoir by Edward D. Hoch. 2004. Cloth, $29.00.

The Danger Zone and Other Stories by Erle Stanley Gardner, edited by Bill Pronzini. 2004.

Dr. Poggioli: Criminologist by T.S. Stribling, edited by Arthur Vidro. 2004. Cloth, $29.00.

The Couple Next Door: Collected Short Mysteries by Margaret Millar, edited by Tom Nolan. 2004.

Sleuth's Alchemy: Cases of Mrs. Bradley and Others by Gladys Mitchell, edited by Nicholas Fuller. 2004.

Who Was Guilty? Two Dime Novels by Philip S. Warne/Howard W. Macy, edited by Marlena E. Bremseth. 2004. Cloth, $29.00. Trade softcover, $19.00.

Slot-Machine Kelly by Dennis Lynds writing as Michael Collins, introduction by Robert J. Randisi. Cloth, $29.00. 2004. Trade softcover, $19.00.

The Evidence of the Sword by Rafael Sabatini, edited by Jesse F. Knight. 2006.

The Casebook of Sidney Zoom by Erle Stanley Gardner, edited by Bill Pronzini. 2006.

The Detections of Francis Quarles by Julian Symons, edited by John Cooper. 2006. Cloth, $29.00.

The Trinity Cat and Other Mysteries by Ellis Peters (Edith Pargeter), edited by Martin Edwards and Sue Feder. 2006.

The Grandfather Rastin Mysteries by Lloyd Biggle, Jr., edited by Kenneth Lloyd Biggle and Donna Biggle Emerson. 2007. Cloth, $29.00. Trade softcover, $19.00.

Masquerade: Ten Crime Stories by Max Brand, edited by William F. Nolan. 2007. Cloth, $29.00. Trade softcover, $19.00.

Dead Yesterday and Other Mysteries by Mignon G. Eberhart, edited by Rick Cypert. 2007. Cloth, $30.00.

The Battles of Jericho by Hugh Pentecost, introduction by S.T. Karnick. 2008. Cloth, $29.00. Trade softcover, $19.00.

The Minerva Club, The Department of Patterns and Other Stories by Victor Canning, edited by John Higgins. 2009. Cloth, $29.00. Trade softcover, $19.00.

The Casebook of Gregory Hood by Anthony Boucher and Denis Green, edited by Joe R. Christopher. 2009. Cloth, $29.00. Trade softcover, $19.00.

Murder at the Stork Club and Other Stories by Vera Caspary, edited by A.B. Emrys. 2009.

Appleby Talks About Crime by Michael Innes, edited by John Cooper. 2010. Cloth, $28.00. Trade softcover, $18.00.

Ten Thousand Blunt Instruments by Philip Wylie, edited by Bill Pronzini 2010. Cloth, $29.00. Trade softcover, $19.00.

The Exploits of the Patent Leather Kid by Erle Stanley Gardner, edited by Bill Pronzini. 2010. Cloth, $29.00. Trade softcover, $19.00.

The Duel of Shadows: The Extraordinary Cases of Barnabas Hildreth by Vincent Cornier, edited by Mike Ashley. 2011. Cloth, $28.00.

The Casebook of Jonas P. Jonas and Other Mysteries by E. X. Ferrars, edited by John Cooper. 2012. Cloth, $29.00. Trade softcover, $19.00.

Night Call and Other Stories of Suspense by Charlotte Armstrong, edited by Rick Cypert and Kirby McCauley. 2014. Cloth, $30.00. Trade softcover, $20.00.

Chain of Witnesses: The Cases of Miss Phipps by Phyllis Bentley, edited by Marvin Lachman. 2015. Cloth, $29.00. Trade softcover, $19.00.

The Puzzles of Peter Duluth by Patrick Quentin. Introduction by Curtis Evans. 2016. Cloth, $29.00. Trade softcover, $19.00.

The Purple Flame and Other Stories of Detection by Frederick Irving Anderson, edited by Benjamin F. Fisher. 2016. Forthcoming.

SUBSCRIPTIONS

Subscribers agree to purchase each forthcoming publication, either the Regular Series or the Lost Classics or (preferably) both. Collectors can thereby guarantee receiving limited editions, and readers won't miss any favorite stories. Subscribers receive a discount of 20% off the list price (and the same discount on our backlist) and a specially commissioned short story by a major writer in a deluxe edition as a gift at the end of the year.

The point for us is that, since customers don't pick and choose which books they want, we have a guaranteed sale even before the book is published, and that allows us to be more imaginative in choosing short story collections to issue. That's worth the 20% discount for us.